W
G

Santa's Greastest Pursuit

Irene Zulueta

Santa's Greatest Pursuit
Irene Zulueta

Published by Winlock Publishing Co.
26135 Murrieta Rd.
Sun City, Ca 92585
(951)943-0014

ISBN 1-890461-51-2

Associate Editor: Hal Lingerman

Editorial assistance: Dave Galey

Cover design and Illustrations: Dave Galey

Price: $14.95

CONTENTS

ULTIMATE RESULTS

CHAPTER ONE

Arriving happily back in Santa Land, Margaret and Santa felt a rest was imminent before they started the first phase of their final pursuit. Margaret was thinking puppies while Santa was thinking about Santa's Airways Group and the hiring of men to play Santa Claus.

Consequently, there would be no rest in sight; time was of the essence and dragging their feet would be unthinkable. They needed to hire at least one man before the holiday season began to replace Santa, should there be a need.

With what seemed to be a never ending summer in Ireland, and no chores with which to be burdened, Leon and Phillip, Nancy and Mildred returned with the group to Santa Land.

Perhaps they had some ideas or suggestions on how the hiring of one man to take his place could be handled. Having the group in this location enabled Santa the opportunity of having discussions with them when it was necessary.

Coming up with a solution to deal with this situation, Leon and Phillip suggested interviewing six men that would compete with one another and they would then choose the one showing the most promise.

This of course meant returning to Ireland to place an ad in the newspaper.

Having the balance of July through September to refine the outline of a Santa Program, Fred and Donald came up with what they thought was the best idea; one man to replace Santa if need be. This allowed them to think one person properly trained could be the man to head and set up the entire program. Together the men, Leon, Phillip, Fred, Donald, Alex and Santa began working on the advertisement to be placed in the newspaper back in Ireland, with Nancy taking notes.

Sitting around the table, putting words on paper, made it look as if it was going to be a cinch to do, as they came up with 'HELP WANTED'. At this point, they sat and looked at one another, not certain what to write after the two 'HELP WANTED' words.

From Fred's mouth came the next addition . . ., " 'MEN INTERESTED' in working on the development of a 'Look-a-Like' Santa Claus . . ."

Interrupting, Donald suggested they change 'HELP WANTED' to 'NOW HIRING MEN TO PLAY SANTA CLAUS AT CHRISTMAS TIME'. Phillip and Leon mentioned that if they were going to hire men, they would have to pay them; so the next thought was to change the words, 'NOW HIRING' to 'VOLUNTEERS WANTED'; then if Santa decided to employ them, depending on their skills, he could discuss compensation at a later date. "I wouldn't even suggest the possibility of this leading to a major position," said Phillip.

Thinking over the idea that had just been presented, Santa and the others thought it was good advice.

The final advertisement read:

VOLUNTEERS WANTED

Men with the desire to become a Look-a-Like
Santa Claus are needed at special Promotions
to be held in the Christmas Season.

All training provided, experience with children
necessary, age irrelevant.

Send Resume's to:

SANTAS AIRWAYS GROUP
137 Hoopla Street
Makover, Ireland

Leon and Phillip applauded the combination of words to be used and Santa was appreciative of the efforts made so far by all, but then without a doubt in his mind remarked, "Now comes the hard part . . . designing the program which will enable the man we choose to become Santa. Just look at me," he proclaimed. "I'm sixty seven years old; do we really want to hire a sixty-seven year old or will perhaps a sixty year old do?"

Trying to exert his importance Fred suggested, "Why don't we compromise and go for the ages of between sixty-three and sixty-eight if at all possible."

Voicing an approval of the age limit, Alex remarked, "That sounds good to me. By the time a man is sixty-three, he should have been able to develop his poise . . . hopefully, has had experience with children . . . and his demeanor should take precedence, especially if he's wearing a red Santa suit. One necessary thing he should possess is the talent to be a good listener, as well as, adept at handling and answering questions properly."

Agreeing with all that was described, Donald inquired about patience and answering him Santa said, "Patience, more than any other attribute is a necessity because without it, most will have a hard time succeeding. So far, so good," commented Santa, "but how do you guys feel about lunch?"

Never wanting to refuse a timeout for lunch, Fred admitted he was famished, and Santa said, "How about quitting for now? Put on your thinking caps and let's resume this meeting tomorrow in my office!" With this compromise, Santa went looking for Margaret to tell her of the progress they'd made.

Finding Margaret in her new office, drawing up what appeared to be a job application, he announced to her that it was lunchtime. Admitting she was hungry and like Santa with his group, wasn't getting too much on paper with the exception of the usual questions like . . . Name . . . Address . . . City and Country, Age and Experience, Margaret agreed to have lunch.

Looking at what she had put down on paper, Santa suggested perhaps he would help her make up the balance of the form after they had eaten.

Welcoming an opportunity to take a break, Margaret and Santa found their way to the kitchen.

Removing a big bowl of vegetable soup from the refrigerator, Margaret transferred it to a medium stock pot, heated it on the stove and filled bowls with soup for each of them.

Their conversation led to Mitzi, Snapper and Mewpurr. According to Margaret's description, the three animals had become bosom buddies in their new home and there was nothing to do but wait for the delivery of Mitzi's puppies; heaven only knew when they would arrive. "This time," Margaret commented, "maybe I can make better preparations."

Finishing their meal, Margaret picked up the empty bowls, rinsed them in the sink and set them on the counter to dry. Santa just sat and watched her every move; he loved this girl he had married so many years ago and never regretted his actions.

Thinking of the application yet to be finished, Santa suggested they give it to Leon and Phillip to complete. They had a pretty good idea of what was needed and he told Margaret, "Hon, if the fellows take on this job, it will leave you free for other things. Perhaps you would like to give more thought to your business, and . . . with Mitzi's puppies on the way you know you'll have your hands full." Knowing Santa had her best interests at heart, Margaret agreed to let him pass the project on to Leon, Phillip, Fred and Donald.

After agreeing with Santa, she brought up an old subject, namely the adventure of restarting the business she had suggested to Dorothy; but to what point would she return. . . where did she leave off? Her memory was beginning to elude her, but Margaret knowing it wouldn't be long before she was back on track thought, maybe another trip to Ireland was what they needed.

Explaining to Santa all of the subjects that put her in a

quandary he said to her, "Remember Hon, one step at a time. That's what I tell Alex and, you too will share in the results of an experience waiting to happen."

Being a patient person, Margaret while remaining a bit confused, once again agreed with Santa.

Since a visit was due in the barn to check on Mitzi's condition, she asked Santa to come along. Much to their surprise, when they approached the stall where the three animals maintained their residence they found five newly born puppies nursing away to their heart's content.

It took Santa no time at all to remind Margaret that having her hands full was not going to happen, as Mitzi was taking care of the puppies all by herself.

Asking, "So what's next?" Margaret listened as Santa suggested, "Hon, why don't you think about teaching Jayne to play the harpsichord. You know how she loves that instrument . . . and then there's also something else we could take into consideration. If you do or don't recall, let me refresh your memory.

Picture the great performance The Entertaining Elvestos gave." Santa went on telling Margaret, "You know, having them entertain for our Christmas trip to Ireland. . ., that's all well and good. Selling their program to anyone in other parts of the country, unless I'm going along is not probable.

Frankly, I really don't want to travel any further than the Toy Thrillers Store so, why don't we think about exploring the suggestion which Fred and Donald mentioned. Allow Jayne along with Jean and Joan, Bernard and Edward, Patrick and Gerald to put an act together. We could promote it and that might give them some sort of income for their future."

Telling Santa, "The reasoning behind the idea sounds great but" Margaret went on, "still . . ., I question whether or not the children would agree to this promotion, which leads to the aspect of another meeting; that of the parents as well as the participants, since their cooperation along with their parent's permission is needed for the possibility to take place." Margaret then implied, "Again, providing the group agrees."

Margaret's imagination raced ahead as she pictured Mary's and Dorothy's faces upon receipt of this proposal. Would they acknowledge this concept with acceptance or totally disapprove of it?

Discussing which method they should attempt, Santa and Margaret decided another dinner with all members of the family in attendance would be appropriate.

Margaret agreed to take the initiative of inviting the two families to dinner the next day while she and Santa put their heads together, working out an approach to a plan that would produce . . .

ULTIMATE RESULTS

HANDLING THE ENTERTAINMENT PROMOTION

CHAPTER TWO

The next day Santa reminded himself that he had adjourned yesterdays meeting with a recommendation of continuing it today in his offices; but he had forgotten to give them the time of day when it would reconvene.

Finishing breakfast, Santa told Margaret, since he'd neglected to mention a time for the affair, he'd better get down there to be available if anyone showed up.

With Santa going out the door, Margaret was left to do as she pleased so she took it upon herself to visit the animals in the barn. Gathering food for them, she was certain they would be hungry; only the newborns had a supply of nourishment ready and waiting to fill their appetites.

Since there was no one available to tell of the puppies arrival, and Margaret felt Patrick would want to know, she sauntered up to visit with Dorothy and Mary hoping to find him.

Margaret's visit with Dorothy and Mary was usually an enjoyable transfer of thoughts and ideas but this time, while telling them of the five new puppies, she was careful not to divulge the purpose for which she was inviting the two families to dinner; that explanation would have to wait until this evening.

After having graciously accepted her invitation to dinner, Margaret asked about Patrick and was told he had gone to the barn. He wanted to make certain Mitzi, knowing of her condition, was being properly attended to. How surprised he was going to be when he found five new puppies.

Bidding the girls adieu, she went to the barn where she found Patrick. As he saw Margaret come through the door, and she heard him practically cooing over the puppies, he said to her, "Have you seen them Aunt Margaret . . . aren't they beautiful?"

Responding, she told him, "Actually they're a work of art to behold Patrick . . . God did a great job when he created them."

Inquisitively, he asked, "Do you suppose Snapper is the father?"

Answering, Margaret specified, "Well, it's hard to tell Patrick, we'll have to wait another few weeks before we can see any similarities . . . But it's always a possibility."

By this time Margaret decided she had better leave and told Patrick he could stay as long as he wanted, but she had other matters which needed her attention, and she would see him later. Without telling him 'later' meant her dinner arrangement for both families, she left the barn.

Returning to the kitchen she began thinking about a choice entree'; but what would it be this time, she wondered.

Going to the freezer Margaret chose some chuck steak with which she could produce a huge pot of San Marco Steak, served over linguine accompanied by a green salad and crescent rolls. That would be easiest for a crowd of thirteen. For dessert she would make a Lush Plus Angel Food Cake, and perhaps offer the adults an after dinner drink. With all of the preparation complete, Margaret decided to fetch Santa from what appeared to be an all day meeting.

Finding him napping in his office, she rapped lightly on his desk to wake him, and his eyes opened. Not expecting to see her and feeling sheepish about his routine he asked, "Did I miss lunch again?"

Not wanting to embarrass him Margaret simply commented, "I thought you wanted to skip lunch, so I bypassed your absence and everything is ready for tonight's dinner with the Gilpatrick's and O'Hares. Jokingly, she added, "I do hope you are going to join us!"

"Why of course. Margaret," answered Santa. "You can't play both Chef and Master of Ceremonies!"

Trying to rush Santa along, she told him she invited them for five o'clock, and it was almost that time now, they'd better hurry.

Having arrived home simultaneously with their guests, Santa did not have time to give her a rundown on what had transpired at his meeting; but did say he would fill her in a little later.

Seeing Dorothy and Mary dressed for dinner, Margaret excused herself so she could do a quick change of clothing to help make her appearance look as if she fit the scene.

While she was gone, Fred began discussing the topics of

today's meeting, thus alerting the women to what he felt was something about to happen . . . something very prominent for the children. Santa had evidently forgotten once again, to ask them not to mention anything to their wives regarding the results of the meeting; at least not until he had discussed it with Margaret. Talking to himself, he said, "I'd better tell Margaret about this," and went looking for her.

Finding Margaret in their bedroom he complimented her, saying, "Margaret, you look so beautiful." For a moment, he'd almost forgotten why he came looking for her but then remembering, he went on to tell her, "Hon, Fred has let the cat out of the bag, and I think he has already told Dorothy with Donald doing likewise, the reason for this get-together. I just thought you should know, so we are both aware of what we are getting into.

At any rate Hon, I'll let you do the talking; you know as well as I what we are trying to achieve."

Margaret felt she knew what Santa was implying, so she firmly planted his words in her mind and said to Santa as she took his arm to join their guests, "Shall we proceed?"

As they entered the room where the Gilpatricks and O'Hares were conversing, Margaret announced, "We're back . . . shall we move on to the dining room?"

As everyone took their seats, Margaret noticed how tall the children were growing.

Motioning over her shoulder to Dolores and Mildred, her helpers for the evening, Margaret had them bring in the food after they said grace; Santa did the honors of pouring wine for everyone as Dolores set their salads in front of them. Next Mildred appeared with the linguine as Dolores entered with bowls of steak combined with a carefully blended sauce and set them on the table.

While everyone was busy devouring their delightful entree' Margaret continued to watch the children. They appeared to be growing up before her eyes. Fred and Donald certainly had the right idea when they mentioned turning them into performers; they definitely had the good looks so often associated with entertainment. However, Margaret thought, maybe I'm getting ahead of myself.

So, rather than staring at the children, Margaret tried to start a conversation beginning with asking Dorothy what she thought about the subjects of the meeting Santa held today.

Responding, Dorothy replied, "That depends on which subject we're talking about. . . I understand there were several."

Not knowing where to go with that answer, Margaret decided to ask another question and inquired, "Well . . . why don't you pick the subject which interests you most."

Thank heavens Santa clued me in on what is happening, thought Margaret, and she went on waiting for Dorothy to give her a response.

Being a manipulator, somewhat like Fred, Dorothy looked at Mary and asked her, "Which subject did you think is most important in the line of order for consideration Mary?"

Understanding Dorothy's deviousness, she came up with what she felt would extract a conclusion. "Well, I would say the most important subject would be the hiring of a Santa Claus because without a Santa to help the business grow, there is no business."

Mary knew what Dorothy was getting at, but she wasn't going to give in to her fantasy, at least not just yet; so the first topic for discussion was the hiring of a look-a-like Santa, and the completion of an application to be filled out by the men answering the newspaper ad.

The children seemed to be paying close attention to all that was being discussed; everything seemed to be business . . . business . . . and more business.

Waiting for an opportune moment to interrupt Jayne saw it and she quickly jumped into the conversation with, "Well folks, now that you have the business running smoothly when are you going to discuss your 'Entertainment Promotion'?"

Quiet grew over the entire room and again Jayne said, "Did you forget about your 'Entertainment Promotion'?"

At this point Mary took it upon herself to voice the answer. "No, Darling, that was without a doubt the next and last subject to be announced . . .but tell us why don't you . . . that is, exactly what do you know or understand about the topic?"

For a moment, Jayne hesitated, thinking she was being too outspoken. To the surprise of all, she came up with, "Maybe it would be better if Aunt Margaret would explain how she would like to handle this portion of the operation. After all, Aunt Margaret is the leader . . ., we are the followers."

Mary was busy thinking, and I thought Dorothy was manipulative; it must run in the family.

Being thankful for Jayne's interpretation as well as her vision regarding her mother's personality, Margaret asked while telling Jayne at the same time, "Evidently, you have several thoughts on this matter sweetheart, so, why don't you tell us what you know about entertaining and that which you feel would be a direct approach to . . .

HANDLING THE ENTERTAINMENT

BACK TO IRELAND

CHAPTER THREE

Because Fred had already told Jayne about his suggestion to Santa regarding the idea of an entertainment promotion, she was all gung ho and ready to answer whatever would promote her calling! However, she had not yet explained the proposition to Jean and Joan or the boys, so she had no idea what their feelings might be when she came up with a solution to the problem.

Choosing her words very carefully, Jayne started out with her understanding of what 'The Entertainment Promotion' was all about. Expounding she said, "I'm certain you guys are aware of the revue performance the 'Entertaining Elvestos' gave, not only at the festival but at The Toy Thrillers Store when Santa put his project on a trial basis. Mr. Tankeroo was so happy with the outcome, he has asked Santa to repeat his performance at Christmas along with the entertainers.

Now, all is well and good for Mr. Tankeroo, but let's face it; this promotion was put on trial in July to see if it would be feasible in the future, namely in the season of Christmas.

Being successful as it was in July, means my dad as well as yours can go out and sell it to other toy stores. The only problem is, Santa, while he will appear this year at The Toy Thrillers Store, along with our Entertaining Elvestos, said he is getting too old to be traveling all over the country to promote his project.

Consequently, this is why we have to develop a look-a-like Santa to take his place in other parts of the world.

Mr. Tankeroo asked if the entertainers would be included along with Santa? While the Entertaining Elvestos agreed, here's where we come in!

If the seven of us can get an act together, we can hire ourselves out as performers to go along with the look-a-like Santa and perhaps pick up some extra income.

There," said Jayne, "I've given you a description of what the 'Entertainment Promotion' is all about."

Complementing Jayne and professing her sincerity Margaret added, "Sweetheart, I couldn't have described it half as well as you did," and directing her thoughts to her guests Margaret asked, "Do we have any comments, constructive criticism or suggestions?"

Knowing of her daughter's enthusiasm Dorothy asked Jayne, "And what kind of package do you propose to develop?"

Pondering an answer to this question, Jayne quite appropriately told her mother, "I suppose if we all want to proceed down this path . . ., and I have yet to ask the others to give me their opinion, we will have to get together to check our talents to find a common denominator, to consider what we can produce!"

This was not the answer Dorothy was expecting, but having been surprised by Jayne's explanation, decided she'd better quit while she was ahead; a decision for which Jayne was grateful.

Next as Jayne called her group by name, Patrick, Gerald,

Bernard and Edward, Jean and Joan, she asked, "What do you guys think . . . are you convinced we can handle it?"

Being the first to speak up, Joan cast a positive thought giving her an affirmative answer, saying, "I don't know why not . . .look at what we accomplished when Rex taught us his gymnastic routines," but Jayne added, "You are right Joan, but I don't believe there would be enough room on the stage to promote this kind of production so, why don't we all put our heads together and see what we can come up with. I'm sure a few of you can sing and Bernard, you play the guitar don't you? Edward, you play the harmonica . . . so what do you say . . . are we on? All in favor say, aye!"

Matching Jayne's enthusiasm a solid concentrated, "Aye" was heard and she knew they could develop their very own winning team.

In Jayne's thoughts, all they needed was a dynamite name but she also knew, between the seven of them they would certainly be able to come up with one.

Without a doubt, Jayne was the star of this affair.

Margaret and Santa felt content, and decided this was the best approach to solve not exactly a problem, but to be able to involve everyone in a project, for the good of humanity.

Santa was busy pouring after dinner drinks and cake appeared on everyone's plate as the dinner neared its end. The night was beginning to gather dust and they all decided it was time to call it a day.

Jayne confirmed that they would have a meeting in a few days, as being out of school afforded them the opportunity to be in a productive mode for the summer vacation, but the main purpose was to be in a creative mood for handling the entertainment.

Having had a successful dinner, once again Santa couldn't wait to tell Alex and the Executive Committee what had taken place. It looked as if they would be on their way back to Ireland in a short time. There was work to be done and wasting time with the few months left before Christmas, was not an option.

Furthermore, the children would soon be returning to school. If they prepared the basics in Santa Land, they could continue fine-tuning the elements of their program after school began.

Santa and Margaret slept peacefully that night, knowing their problems for the time had a solution. When they awoke in the morning, their conversation at breakfast centered on the schedule they would have to prepare, not only for traveling to Ireland, but placing the ad in the newspaper to interview and train the men, as well as, the development of a program.

Telling Margaret, "It looks as if my work is cut out for me," and he added, "I do hope it's all manageable!"

Complimenting him, Margaret remarked, "Hon, if anyone can do it, you can." Thanking her for a vote of confidence Santa left to look for Alex. Finding him along with Leon and Philip in the Conference Room over the post office, working with Fred and Donald, he felt like an intruder, even as they welcomed him.

"Am I interrupting anything?" inquired Santa.

Speaking up Fred answered, "No, we hoped we would be able to finish this project as a surprise for you, but since you're here, you might as well join us."

Replying, Santa inquired, "And with what is it you are trying to surprise me?"

"Well," replied Leon, "we thought you might like to see the finished program we have designed to train the man or men who you decide are worthy of becoming a look-a-like Santa."

This news delighted him to no end as he questioned their project.

Donald taking the lead explained to Santa all about the interviews.

"If we can concentrate on their ability to behave as you did with the children, training them should be no problem. We feel that Alex's suggestion regarding age, between sixty-five and sixty-eight would be just right, but then, there is the problem of size. Because you are the original model, and you looked so great in your red suit and hat, your image is the one we will always have in our minds when we start interviewing. At the same time, we don't want to discourage anyone from helping us out because he can't meet the criteria . . ."

Santa stopped him right in the middle of his explanation, informing him, "Donald, I think you are way ahead of yourself. Maybe we had better get the help wanted advertisement in the newspaper and see what kind of applicants apply for our promotion. It might make all the difference in the world if we should just happen to find a man talented enough to take over the whole project, so all you have to do is sell it.

I'll tell you what we should do, and that is . . . Let's head back to Ireland and get that ad in the paper. Until we actually have applicants lining up at our door, it will be hard to know in which direction we are traveling. Consequently, I suggest we return to Ireland by the end of this week; that should give us enough time to get some details on paper. We already know the age of the man we want, but my next question is, how are we going to train him? What are we going to tell him about our experiment? Will he be agreeable . . . will he think we're nuts? Or maybe, he will be someone who has read about us in the July news and thinks he would like to join our efforts or . . . perhaps he has something to offer us; but before anything can happen, we will have to get that ad in the paper, and I say . . . let's do it now!"

Everyone sat and listened as Santa made quite clear what it was he wanted. There was no debating Santa, he was back on track and all they could do was go along with his line of thinking. Adjourning the get-together, everyone departed the Conference Room and went home to begin making plans for another trip . . .

BACK TO IRELAND

NEW PLANS

CHAPTER FOUR

Racking her brain to figure out a catchy name for the entertainment group about to be formed, Jayne decided she would need the help of those involved. She wanted to think she could do it herself, but try as she may, nothing seemed to arouse her imagination.

With time to spare, she contacted the other members to alert them of a get together, telling them they would meet in the Conference Room the next morning to discuss their talents; that is, providing the room wasn't being used.

After asking Bernard to bring his guitar and Edward his harmonica, she had only the day left to come up with a name for their act, but maybe she was trying too hard.

Deciding to allow her brain a bit of relaxation, she hurried on to look for Aunt Margaret, only to learn that she was in the barn checking on Mitzi's puppies; so that's where she went.

To date she'd only heard about the puppies, but had not yet seen them. As she entered the barn, she found her brothers, Patrick and Gerald, each cuddling a puppy while Margaret had two, one in each arm.

Naturally, she thought the one remaining must be for her. Picking up the puppy and holding it lovingly to her cheek, the little one let out a slow stream of gas. "Oh no!" shouted Jayne. "You little Stinker."

Eveyone laughed including Jayne as she remarked, "If it's going to happen, it's going to happen to me."

With all of the laughter going on, no one noticed the turd coming from the puppy Patrick held, until it lay in his lap. Pointing at Patrick, Gerald said, "Look Jayne . . . you have no monopoly on puppy problems."

The laughter continued until the puppy Gerald was holding peed all over him.

Margaret was blushing because, while this incident meant nothing to the children, embarrassingly, her face grew red from one end to the other and Jayne commented, "Well, that's life in puppy land."

Naming the puppy she would like to have Stinker, Jayne heard Patrick say he would name his puppy 'Turdo'; being gentler, Gerald holding one lone puppy named it 'Peepe', a mispronunciation of the name 'Pepe'.

Having two puppies remaining, Margaret was undecided to whom they should go, but time would tell. For now, to all appearances three dogs and one cat traveling back to Ireland, helped Patrick think, he could begin work on the establishment of his very own animal menagerie, but he'd think about that later.

Deciding it was time to leave Jayne's version of puppy land, Margaret accompanied the children out of the barn.

For now, Patrick knowing he had a good voice, decided to help Jayne with the 'Entertainment Promotion' and told her he would see her at the meeting, as he went on to other concerns awaiting his attention.

Meanwhile, with everything moving smoothly along, Jayne again started concentrating on a name for their group. Aloud she said, "Jean, Joan, Jayne . . .," there they are, three of them, three Js . . . three joys . . . three jades . . .," that sounded good to Jayne. She repeated it over several times and then added accompaniment to The Three Jades.

With an announcement of the name one more time, 'The Three Jades & Accompaniment,' she said, "Not quite!"

Abandoning the process of creating a new name, Jayne decided she would wait until tomorrow's meeting to see what ideas the others might have.

Looking for Margaret, Santa forewarned her about packing their bags for another trip to Ireland. Not bothering to ask why, she knew him well enough to know he wouldn't ask her to do something without reason. Hurriedly packing their luggage as if they would be leaving tomorrow, she understood the other wives followed the same request from their husbands; but at this time, she wasn't certain they were going along. Consequently, Margaret said nothing to Dorothy or Mary, she simply waited for them to key her in.

That evening after they had turned in for the night, Santa told Margaret that he suggested Fred's and Donald's families come along as there was a lot of work to be done and he had no idea how long this session would last. Not wanting Mary and Dorothy to remain at home, waiting and possibly worrying about their husband's return, he thought it best for them to go along on the trip.

By taking the children, they would be in a position to see what was being developed in the way of an entertaining promotion which Dorothy and Mary might be able to preview and help organize, should the children desire assistance.

Santa added, "As you know Margaret, Alfred reported the weather to be travel worthy, so I had Alex alert everyone, and we will be off early this morning."

While it was time to sleep, with Santa's explanation of the activity to take place, Margaret realized how much preparation was needed before they could leave.

Since Leon, Phillip, Nancy and Mildred, Fred and Donald along with their wives and children, possibly Alex and Alfred coming too, she found there was no way in which they could bring the animals expected to accompany them. Considering this situation, Margaret knew she had to forewarn someone about their absence and the need to care for her pets while they were gone.

She chose to tell Dolores as Margaret knew she would find someone capable of assisting her, especially since Mildred and Nancy were among the group returning to Ireland. Being readily willing to accept responsibility when Margaret talked to her, Dolores implied she would ask Gloria for some help. That was her choice of recommendation and feeling confident with Dolores' judgment, Margaret went back to bed, but not for long.

Take-off time had rapidly filled the sleigh with passengers

ready to leave. Santa Land was hardly what anyone might call dull. Excitement always seemed to abound, not only in the air, but especially when Santa called, "Let's GO GUYS" as well as a mention of . . . .

NEW PLANS

LOOKING FOR A NEW NAME

CHAPTER FIVE

Having temporarily settled in Ireland with the month of August quickly approaching, waiting for July to move on, the men filled their days with work. Constantly changing their ideas, plans, methods of operation, to all appearances, they finally came to a conclusion, or so they thought.

While the committee was busy sorting out their differences, Jayne was busy with her group. Not having the accommodations available to them as they existed in Santa Land, the decision was to assemble in the barn and, for their purposes, that would be just fine.

Gathering the day after their arrival, Bernard brought his guitar and Edward his harmonica. The only instruments for Patrick and Gerald were their beautiful, harmonizing voices; back in Santa Land they often vocalized in duets. Jean and Joan simply sang along as background singers, and Jayne decided she would do the same.

With all being well and good, Jayne knew it was time to bring up the subject of a name for their group; she suggested 'The Three Jades and Accompaniment' but also insinuated the name wasn't quite right. At this point, Gerald spoke up telling them, "I like the 'Three Jades', but that's for the girls. How about 'The Santaliers' for the boys? After all, coming from Santa Land should have some bearing on the name." Jayne followed up by complimenting his ingenuity and telling him, "I think that is a great addition Gerald; now if we can just arrange the words so they'd give us an appropriate feeling, and then Edward speaking up, contributed, "How about 'Santa's Santaliers'?" Next came Patrick suggesting, 'The Santaliers with Jaded Accompaniment' as their official name, but not quite accepted by all. One more recommendation was offered and the name settled on was, 'The Santaliers with Jaded Accompaniment'.

The explanation presented by Joan regarding the change of name turned out to define the representation of boys or girls that could be either. The girls could be 'Santaliers' and the boys 'Jaded Accompaniment' or vice-versa but with a name like this, it meant they were one.

The next subject would involve the music to be played. Since it was actually going to be the Christmas Season for which they would be entertaining, they settled on a theme of Christmas songs; this would most likely put everyone into the greater spirit of Christmas.

While the group continued to delve into their purpose, Santa was busy meeting with those he called, 'The Salesmen's Executive Committee', comprised of Fred and Donald, along with Leon, Phillip and their secretary, Nancy. Many subjects had yet to be covered and there was little time in which to do this.

Mildred and Margaret were busy poring over recipes and needed groceries while Dorothy and Mary took this opportunity to shop. Their trip took them to the thrift store where Donald and Fred bought the shoes they needed to appear as successful salesman.

Upon entering the door, they were amazed to see the capacity of the inside area. Wandering around the store, Dorothy and Mary took notice of every item and how neatly the merchandise was arranged. They looked at clothing, books, toys, household goods . . . you name it; this store had it. Both Mary and Dorothy decided the next time they were in need of anything, this was the first place they would look. Noticing the clock on the wall, they realized it was getting late, so homeward bound they turned.

As the Executive Committee ended their meeting, they felt that they had taken care of quite a bit of detail, many loose ends and were ready for action. Fred and Donald would take the advertising to be placed in the newspaper down to the proper authority tomorrow. Of course they asked Santa to come along as he would have to pay for the cost of the ad and they had no money of which to speak.

Margaret had returned from grocery shopping early enough to allow Mildred adequate time to prepare dinner for the large group.

Returning from visiting friends in the forest, Alex and Alfred beckoned the children to join them as it was dinnertime.

Everyone sat down to what appeared to be a feast, said grace and started clamoring over who wanted what. Evidently, they all had busy schedules that day and having spent their energy, had humungous appetites to feed.

Conversation wise, Dorothy asked Jayne if they had accomplished anything regarding, as she put it, their common denominator? Jayne's answer to her mother told her about the development of a name for their group which she hoped Santa would like. Telling her the name was 'The Santaliers and Jaded Accompaniment', Dorothy didn't hesitate to give Jayne her opinion, regarding the sound of the name; she suggested it was too long.

Thinking about what she said, Jayne all at once, realized 'The Jaded Accompaniment' should be dropped and using only 'The Santaliers' would be best. Complimenting her mother for providing the essence of professionality, Jayne told her, "I'll discuss it with the others, and I know they'll love it."

As everyone sat at the table, it turned out to be a not so private conversation, and when they heard 'The Santaliers', Joan perked up and said, "I think your mom is right Jayne, 'The Jaded Accompaniment' should be dropped . . . I really like 'The Santaliers' – all by itself." Gerald adding to the speculation agreed saying, "It was there all the time. Maybe we were trying too hard . . . My vote goes for . . . 'The Santaliers' and everyone cheering, with forks raised high as if to toast 'The Santaliers' meant this was the end of . . .

LOOKING FOR A NEW NAME

A TEAR IN HIS EYE

CHAPTER SIX

Time waited for no one, and as the Executive Committee completed the Christmas advertising, Donald and Fred took it upon themselves to return to The Toy Thrillers Store to get Mr. Tankeroo's approval on the artwork. This material would enable him to reserve space for advertising in the holiday issue and also, to obtain a figure on the cost.

Of course, there would be no charge for the work of the design, and they were certain Mr. Tankeroo would be totally thankful for the time Santa's crew had put into it.

As Fred and Donald entered the premise, they noticed the little boy called Andre' who happened to be wandering around, reviewing various items all about the store.

While this sight appeared to be strange, since neither the cashier nor his mother seemed to be nearby, Fred decided he would befriend the boy and started a conversation with him! Not wanting to frighten him, Fred called out from across the room, "Hello there Andre' . . . how are you today?"

Looking up from the item he was checking out, he answered, "Very good sir . . . And how are you? Did you bring my braces . . . are they ready yet?"

At this point, Fred was almost sorry he had spoken to the boy, but the damage was done and he quickly had to devise an answer so as not to disappoint him. Being disabled was hard enough on the boy without letting him down on the basis of a negative reply.

Standing by, listening to the meager conversation, Donald decided to join in and told him, "No Andre' . . . We haven't brought your braces because Santa had to put in a special order for the material necessary to make them; I'm sure they will be here by Christmas."

When Fred heard this comment, he said to Donald, "How can you tell him that? What if Punky doesn't get the material . . . What then?"

Responding, Donald told Fred, "We'll cross that bridge when we come to it, at Christmas. As a matter of fact, I'm not certain Santa even asked Punky about the braces . . . a mere oversight!"

As Fred inquired regarding the whereabouts of Mr. Tankeroo, Andre' offered, "I'll get him for you and, before Fred could say "No . . . wait . . . ," Andre' took off unlike a boy with crutches, but more like a flash of lightening, while calling loudly, "Grandpa . . ., Grandpa . . ., come quickly . . . Fred and Donald are here to see you!"

Hearing the boy calling "Grandpa . . . Grandpa . . .," and ignoring the rest of his statement, Mr. Tankeroo quickly came from the back room thinking it was an emergency.

Seeing Fred and Donald waiting at the door, his face brightened and he invited the men in while saying, "Welcome back Fred and you too, Donald, it's good to see you again; to what do we owe the pleasure of this visit?"

Realizing Mr. Tankeroo had evidently forgotten about the advertising, they promised to execute for The Toy Thrillers Store, Fred took the papers from his briefcase and asked if they could use his office where they would have more privacy.

Leading them back to his room and taking seats in the chairs provided, Fred and Donald spread open their papers on Mr. Tankeroo's desktop.

Inquiring what this might be, Donald told Mr. Tankeroo this was the advertising for the Christmas Program to begin at the end of November.

Evidently, Mr. Tankeroo had forgotten about the ads they would furnish and after seeing the finished product he asked, "Do you think this project will be very expensive?"

Answering his question, Donald proclaimed, "There's no charge for the art work; the only expense will have to be for the placement of the ads in the newspaper after you have reserved the space. We will take care of the details, as Santa originally offered."

Hesitating, Mr. Tankeroo sat back, wondering how he could afford all of this. Business had not been too swift, and most of the funds he had reaped in July were gone. He had paid his cashier back wages and ordered some new stock as well as ornaments, which were always a good seller. Not wanting to incur another debt, he told the men, "I'll have to think about this one. Since there is still time to reserve space, I'll have to figure out exactly where I stand financially.

If it is at all feasible, I will arrange for the reservation and confirm it with you at the time, but tell me, will Santa be back with the Elvestos, or are you planning a look-a-like Santa?"

Wondering about the reason for this question Donald told Mr. Tankeroo that to date, while the help wanted advertising was ready for publication, they had not yet placed it in the newspaper. To all appearances, Santa wanted to do the job himself; and yes, the Entertaining Elvestos will be performing.

Seeing that their work at the toy store was finally finished Fred stated, "Well Mr. Tankeroo, if you have no further comments, our work here is complete, so we will be on our way, anxiously awaiting to hear from you."

Mr. Tankeroo walked Fred and Donald to the door and, waving goodbye to Andre' as they left the store, Fred and Donald engaged themselves in conversation regarding the relationship between Andre' and Mr. Tankeroo.

"What do you think about this development, Fred?" asked Donald. Replying as if he were looking through a Fortune Teller's Glass Ball, Fred exclaimed, "I'll tell you what I think, Donald." He went on to say . . . "We already know Mr. Tankeroo is Andre's grandfather, and I'll bet you, Beverly, the cashier, is Andre's mother, making her Mr. T's daughter. It's no wonder you saw . . .

A TEAR IN HIS EYE"

THE HIRING PROCESS

CHAPTER SEVEN

The next question to Santa from Fred was, "How long do you suppose we'll be staying in Ireland?"

Puzzling over this inquiry, Santa replied, "Well, that depends on how many men answer our advertisement and we haven't even put the ad in the paper. Maybe, rather than waiting till tomorrow, we could do it today.

After the advertising appears in print, we'll have to wait for men to connect with it. Maybe we should change the ad just a bit, stating a time when they can come to our door to apply for this position. We'll have to set up a room where they can fill out their application, as well as finding out when they'll be available for an interview.

I'll tell you what," said Santa. "Why don't we put the ad in the newspaper today. Then we can come home, and together we can make a list of how to process each man with his application."

"That sounds good to me," commented Donald, and Fred agreed.

With this decision, the three men corrected the advertising write up. Finding Margaret in the kitchen, they told her they were off to the post office, so she would know of their whereabouts.

Going out the door, the men made their way to the "Help Wanted" section of the newspaper office. Seeing no line at the counter, they found themselves being waited on by an agent asking if he could help them. Removing the papers from his briefcase, Fred presented them to the clerk.

Looking at the ad the men were trying to place, the representative, with a grin on his face inquired, "Do you people belong to an actor's group?"

Waiting to be told the cost of the advertisement, Santa questioned, "And why do you ask?"

Responding, the clerk told him, "Well, look at your ad sir. You are looking for volunteers; this means there is no pay. Do you think men want to work for free?"

Foreseeing a problem with this man, Santa abruptly answered, "Are you telling me we cannot place the ad in the Help Wanted Section because we are looking for volunteers?"

Realizing he had no right to refuse this advertisement and yet disputing its content, the representative told the men he would have to check with his supervisor to see if he could accept it for publication, considering its nature.

Growing irritated, Santa told him, "Well do it and do it quickly, we don't have all day!"

Fred and Donald, eyeing Santa's disposition had no idea he could be so powerful when he wasn't getting what he wanted. As they waited for the agent to reappear, they heard Santa muttering under his breath to himself, "He must think we are some kind of cult . . . I wonder what kind of idiot he is."

Returning to the counter, the clerk gave him a price for running the ad. Curtailing his behavior, Santa paid the clerk and politely thanked the representative as he assured him the ad would appear in print for the next three days.

Leaving the newspaper office, the three men returned home and sat at the table, ready to plot their plan of action, hopefully beginning the next day. Speaking first, Fred commented, "I have given this situation much thought and," he went on, "as you know there is not too much space in this house. What will we do if we have . . . let's say a dozen men answering our advertising, all on the same day?"

Tilting his head, Santa remarked, "You have a good point Fred."

Listening to the two of them, Donald offered his suggestion of what seemed to be a logical solution. "If we make up an appointment schedule and give each man an application to be completed and brought back the next day, at his appointed time, we can end our interviewing in three days, no more than four. After reviewing each application we can tell them they will be notified by mail. At least that will save them from the embarrassment of having been turned down."

"Great idea," said Fred, "Now . . . how many applications do we have available?"

Agreeing with this solution, Santa told them to check with

Nancy for the count and also to ask her to make up a workable appointment schedule.

It looked as if they had finally accomplished something enabling them to complete the beginning of a not so easy process.

Awakening the next day, Santa could hardly wait to look through the paper for their advertisement. Fred and Donald joined him, peering over his shoulder as he flipped through the pages that led to the Help Wanted Ads.

There it was in big bold print - - - 'VOLUNTEERS WANTED'

"Well" said Santa, "they certainly did a good job of placing the advertisement in a visible spot. All we have left to do is to wait and, as the men show up, give them each an application to be filled out, assign a time for them to return and evaluate their qualifications after they leave."

While everyone expected the doorbell to be ringing off the wall, nothing took place. Of course, it was very early in the morning. Finally, realizing nothing would occur until after breakfast, Santa decided to embark upon a trip to the barn to check on the reindeer; with Donald and Fred following close behind.

Finding that all was quiet and everyone still dozing, Santa motioned to the two that he was returning to the kitchen where he would put on the coffee. As they opened the door they found Mildred and Margaret already in the process of preparing breakfast.

Speaking to the group Margaret uttered, "Welcome to another day guys," and nonchalantly Fred answered, "You too!"

Pouring several cups of coffee, Margaret carried them to the table as she asked, "What's on the agenda for today Santa?"

He told her their schedule would depend on how many men might show up to apply for the job, which had just been advertised. Margaret then proceeded to ask Santa how he felt about the advertisement.

Telling her of their experience regarding the agent at the newspaper office, she reminded him of the facts. "Hon, you'll have to remember, not everyone is aware of this new approach. Maybe he doesn't even know what took place in July, so . . ." but Santa interrupting to declare his cause said, "Just because he's unaware of Santa Claus's existence doesn't mean he has to think we are a group of weirdos looking for 'Volunteers'."

"Well Hon," Margaret disputed, "Let's face it, who in their right mind would advertise for someone to work for free . . . after all, if one had described oneself as a charitable organization, I'll bet he would have had no problem with your ad." Not expecting this type of reply from Margaret, Santa felt rather disappointed with her decision to take an opponent's side; then he thought, to all appearances, she could be right.

Continuing with her line of thinking, Santa expounded as he asked her, "Do you think we are a charitable organization?"

Answering him, Margaret determined, "In reality, you are, are you not? You are giving gifts to children, you've decided to visit hospitals and orphanages where they did not have these niceties . . . the only problem is . . . you are not known; and besides, you have yet to earn any money from the business you are building. This is a new phase of charity, and it has not yet been completed. It depends on where you take it."

Calming his own disposition, Santa agreed with her, and those sitting and listening on the sidelines, saw the effect Margaret had on Santa.

Finishing breakfast, they heard the familiar sound of the doorbell and sat, anxiously looking at one another. Margaret finally asked if someone had been appointed to answer the door.

Jumping up with an application in hand accompanied by an appointment schedule, Donald left the room. It took him no time at all to give the gentleman calling an application and apply his name to the schedule for the next day. Upon his return, Santa said, "See, I knew there would be someone out there that we could count on," and just as these words left his mouth the doorbell rang again.

Happily, Fred announced, "I'll get it," and this he did. After placing another name on the schedule, he rejoined them.

Santa felt exhilarated, but this high didn't last for long because, wait as they might, the bell didn't ring again for the rest of the day.

Feeling weary, Santa proclaimed, "Well . . . tomorrow's another day, and so much for business."

Trying to comfort Santa that night when they retired, Margaret told him, "Hon, look at the bright side for now; maybe two men are all you can handle. Really, if you take them back to Santa Land, and share with them everything you know about playing Santa Claus, and just what it is you are trying to achieve, you may find another Fred and Donald. After all, do you know where you are going to begin? What is the first thing you will tell them?

You Hon . . . are a natural. You stepped into the role you wanted and dreamt of playing, with no trouble at all; but what are you going to tell them that will allow each one to step in as you did? For now, all they know tells them they have applied for a job as a 'volunteer' to be a look-a-like Santa Claus. Even the children, that is, Jayne and the guys, understand more about Santa Claus than the two men who answered your advertisement.

I think it best we sit down and outline what you want to tell them, about how they can become you; but for now Hon, don't feel dejected . . . it's only a matter of time . . . just like it was from the day you started this project through the finish, when you did what you set out to do at The Toy Thrillers Store. Don't forget, tomorrow's another day."

Dwelling on what Margaret had projected, Santa told her, "Hon, you're right. Tomorrow we'll sit down and put it on paper so we can try to make it happen, and I thank you so much, as you help me to remember . . . 'PERSISTENCE' is the necessary word for . . .

THE HIRING PROCESS"

TOMORROW IS A NEW DAY

CHAPTER EIGHT

Once again, awakening early in the morning, finishing breakfast and awaiting the doorbell to ring, Santa thought to himself, perhaps I'm expecting too much. Maybe I'm a dreamer; and yet Fred and Donald have no problem with my plan. So what can I say when I've said, 'I'm sorry', but 'I'm not sorry'. Everything seems to be going as planned; nevertheless, something seems to be missing . . . "What is missing?" Santa asked himself.

Joining him, Fred and Donald could tell he was discouraged, so they said nothing while just waiting for the doorbell to ring.

Wanting to run off to his office, Santa knew he wasn't in Santa Land and since he did not have this accommodation, maybe he would step out to the barn. He simply wanted to be alone.

Telling Fred and Donald to answer the bell if it rang, Santa explained his need for privacy and quickly left for the place where he knew he'd find Alex.

Luckily, as Santa was exiting the house, Alex stood at the door, ready to enter. Looking at him, Santa said, "I'm so glad you are here Alex, I need to talk."

Alex was not surprised at Santa's disclosure and inquired about a location where they could talk privately. Not knowing many places of seclusion, Santa suggested they walk through the garden.

41

As they walked and talked, Santa said to Alex, "You know, my friend, we have been together for a long time and you have been so helpful . . . but right now, while all seems to be going well, something seems to be missing. Tell me Alex, who is it that gives you so much help? You know, the one who originally sent you to me with all of your friends; the one to whom you turn to ask for help when you think you need it. Do you think he would help me if I asked him?"

Alex knowing he was referring to his friend Gabriel, to be exact the Archangel Gabriel, wasn't quite certain how to answer this question. Santa never forgets the help Gabriel has afforded him, but God, Alex thought, would Gabriel want to get involved in the aspirations of Santa?

While employing his memory, a picture of the word, 'God' flashed through his mind; that was the answer. It was God who had sent the Archangel Gabriel to him, so maybe he should tell Santa that if he needed some help, he should pray to God. If the Archangel Gabriel wasn't the right person to whom he might apply . . . , God could send the correct one for the necessary assistance. All we have to do is believe and pray a whole lot.

Having explained the details of what he wanted to Alex, there was another option about which Santa reminisced.

Remembering the first trip to Ireland, whereas the whole group went to church on the Sunday before they returned home, as well as how much he enjoyed the minister's homily, he never stopped to think of building a church in Santa Land. That's it, he thought; we need a church in Santa Land! As Alex listened, Santa asked, "Do you think you and your comrades could build a church?"

Under his breath Alex uttered, "Oh boy, here we go again," while inquiring of Santa . . . "Well, that depends on how big?"

Picturing the size of the castle Santa commented, "Well it doesn't have to be as large as our living quarters." He hesitated to use the word castle because it was humungous, and he didn't need a church that size. Trying to survey the idea Alex asked Santa, "And once you've built this church, where will you find a minister? Where will you find someone who wants to live in Santa Land? You know, just advertising for a minister is not an option."

Realizing he had not given this subject any thorough thought, Santa remarked to Alex, "Maybe it's not a practical idea, but there must be a solution lurking someplace around the corner," and as he made this suggestion, his memory developed a picture of the church, called, St. Adeline's, that stood around the corner from their house. As a matter of fact it was the church that Margaret attended when she was a child and also where she went to school.

Once again in a dither, Santa being uncertain where to start . . . wasn't even certain Alex knew where to begin.

Returning to the house after having his conversation with Alex, Santa remembered he had two interviews to conduct mid-day.

Only two men so far had the courage to come to the door and volunteer their time to play Santa Claus, and they would be returning early in the afternoon.

Realizing he'd better get down to business, Santa hadn't even begun to outline his method of questioning, and once again, time was flying, so finding Margaret, he asked her to accompany him to his office. Being aware of Santa's intent to draw up the strategy he would use, she readily went along, thinking she could help in his hiring process. Sitting at his desk, they started with what they felt came first, and that was location. Since there were only two men on the list for today, Santa decided to play it by ear, as usual, one step at a time.

First he would explain his intent to them and break down the reasoning behind a Santa Claus and his desire to pursue such a project.

In the process of looking back over his many years, from the time he had delivered the Angel Marion to Bethlehem and the forty years that followed the birth of Jesus Christ, His death, Crucifixion and Resurrection when people began to celebrate and give one another gifts in honor of a day called Christmas, his dream came alive. This was the first item to be conveyed to the men.

Margaret sat and listed Santa's projections in outline form to make it easier for him to follow. First on the list was the 'Reason for the Job'. Next, after reviewing the men's applications, checking out their ages and locale of origin, Santa decided it was necessary to determine if they had any objections to traveling. This would help him decide if the training should be held in Ireland or Santa Land; but, not to forget that eventually they would be traveling to different parts of the country, as Fred and Donald sold his program.

Looking at what was next on the list, Santa would ask them what they thought of his idea. Of course, in Santa's mind, negative answers would immediately disqualify them.

Wanting to ask why the men felt they met his criteria, Santa thought, heaven only knows what the answer to this question might be; but maybe he was on the wrong track. Asking Margaret what she thought, Santa was in total acceptance of her feelings.

Partially agreeing with him on the first question, and even the second one, Margaret felt he should stop after the second answer, but then he might, even go so far as the third part to see if they liked to travel, whether they liked the idea of interviewing children, (so to speak) and also, ask if they had any objection to wearing a red suit, which was soon to be Santa's trademark! After all she added, "You can't be too choosy; remember, these men are volunteers."

Ending with her feedback, Santa said, "You are right Hon; and until we actually talk to them, who knows what, in reality we'll come up with. So . . . , here's how I will conduct myself:

First, I will tell them why I am doing this and next, I will refer to traveling. Then I will ask about their relationship with children.

If they have the right answers, I'll try to train them both at the same time. After all, there's nothing like a back up, and so far there are only two of them."

It wasn't long before the doorbell rang and Margaret went

to answer it. Finding two elderly looking gentlemen, she asked the reason for their visit.

Thinking these were two new men answering Santa's advertisement, she handed them applications and proceeded to put their names on the time schedule when one of the men inquired, "You mean, we have to come back here again?" Being taken aback Margaret, apologized as she inquired, "I'm sorry sir. I didn't get your name; are you already on the Appointment Schedule?"

Answering her question he proclaimed, "My name is Mr. Jiltor. I have completed the paper I was given yesterday and I've returned for my scheduled appointment as I was asked to do, at 2:00."

Embarrassed by her error, Margaret looked at the other man waiting for them to finish their conversation and questioned who he might be?

Answering, he called himself Mr. Egowrap! Then he told her, "I too, have my papers completed and am keeping the appointment given me yesterday for 2:00 today."

"My goodness," commented Margaret, "One of our schedulers must have made a mistake; if you will wait one moment, allow me to check and see if both interviews could be conducted at the same time?" and she left the room.

Telling Santa, "There are two men at the door. It seems as if someone has confused the scheduling, the two men, were asked to complete their applications and were set up for an appointment at the same time."

Knowing these men were the two interviews he was anticipating, Santa thought to himself, that's great. Then telling Margaret to bring him their applications along with asking them to come in, he said, "I can see them both at the same time; which means I would only have to explain the project once. In that way, after it is all over, we can compare one against the other."

Following Santa's instructions, Margaret did as he asked and returned to the two men who were awaiting his interview. She showed them into the living room and sat them before the fireplace where the atmosphere appeared quite comfortable.

Entering the room, Santa sat facing them in a large easy chair. Introducing himself to the two men, he then reviewed their applications. Greeting Mr. Egowrap and Mr. Jiltor, Santa introduced himself as Santa Claus and went on to explain that he was the one who had held the great extravaganza at The Toy Thrillers Store this past July.

Unfortunately, Mr. Jiltor had not heard of this gala event, but Mr. Egowrap had.

When Santa realized Mr. Egowrap had absorbed the occurrence, his first comment was, "That's wonderful!"

Because his first impression was, 'There's a man who understands what I am trying to do', it was time to paint the picture Santa wanted to portray, and he began by expounding . . .

TOMORROW IS A NEW DAY

ST GABRIEL'S ANGELIC REALM

CHAPTER NINE

As Santa was explaining his efforts, both men listened to his story and admitted to his plight being quite challenging. He described the event of the children as they stood before him, requesting a gift or two. Sometimes they would make what seemed to be an inappropriate comment, and yet, they were only children . . . , thus one would overlook the adventuresome trips they were imagining while expressing their wishes.

Viewing the two men's applications, Santa noticed the pair lived very close to the area in which The Toy Thrillers Store was located. Consequently, he asked them if they had by chance patronized the store recently, if ever.

Mr. Jiltor admitted to having no children for whom to shop, while Mr. Egowrap claimed he had a number of nieces and nephews who never seemed to have enough toys. He admitted to Santa, what he had in mind when deciding to volunteer as a Santa Claus; that was, being able to buy toys at a discount in exchange for his good deed. Santa was a little surprised at his point of view, but then, why not, he thought to himself; at least he's honest about his motives.

When Santa proceeded to ask Mr. Jiltor about his outlook, regarding volunteer work, he explained his need to get ahead. Neglecting to ask him how he would do this, Santa accepted his answer. Mr. Jiltor seemed to be more the business oriented type of man with an aspect of succeeding at whatever he tried, and in this case, it was volunteer work.

Santa had a decision to make; as to which of the two men sounded best for the job? Realizing there was still another day of advertisement in the paper to which they might have answers by men willing to volunteer for their cause, Santa asked the men if he could be in touch with them as there might be other applicants to be taken into consideration.

Trying to determine their attitudes about traveling Santa continued, "I will tell you this much. While our volunteer work may begin in this city, our program will take you to other destinations as we continue to grow. There will be other men joining our organization and we will be looking for one specific person to train those who follow.

Depending on how many applicants we receive, we may do the training in Santa Land. Hopefully, you won't mind if we transport you to our village, but if we do not get too many more volunteers, the training may be right here in Ireland."

When Santa asked the men if this was satisfactory, they both mentioned that they preferred not to travel. Of course , this response gave Santa a clue as to the range of their personalities and he decided this would allow him to make a definite decision about handling the matter. Telling the men that he would be in touch with them within the week, Santa bid them farewell as they departed.

The rest of the afternoon was uneventful; not one more applicant came to the door, and eventually, while it saddened Santa to find only two men applying for this position, he made up his mind to be content and work with what he had. Deciding to take a short before dinner nap, Santa found an easy chair much to his liking.

As he napped, Jayne and her group were out in the barn trying to establish some musical habits while practicing the Christmas Hymns they knew so well. First on their list came 'Silent Night', as Bernard with his guitar and Edward with his harmonica combined their talents. Patrick and Gerald harmonized beautifully as the girls hummed along in the background.

Hearing the murmur of music off in the distance, Margaret decided to look for its location. Following the sound, she was led right out the door to the barn area where she had her first glimpse of, 'The Santaliers' in action.

As they continued to sing their first song, Margaret couldn't help but think of how hauntingly, beautiful the 'Silent Night' had become. Having beheld a great presentation being created before her eyes, she quietly returned to the house.

Margaret's imagination came alive, having been prompted by the sound of the music, which filled her head, leading her to remember the beautiful tones she would hear in St. Adeline's Church, which she attended as a child.

It was then she realized what was missing in her life. Until now she'd hardly given it a thought; then she said to herself, "So why am I thinking of this now?" Realizing there was a method to God's goodness, she knew she had to have a discussion with Santa about this new revelation and it couldn't wait; it had to be now.

Looking for Santa, Margaret found him napping. In her anxiety, she woke him to disclose what she was feeling about a new concept. Upon his awakening the first thing Margaret heard

Santa ask was, "Is dinner ready yet?" Knowing it was on its way, she told him, "No dinner isn't ready yet; however, I have something important to discuss with you."

Trying to clear his head, Santa asked Margaret, "Can it wait, or does it have to be now?"

Disappointedly she answered, "Well it's something to think about so the sooner we discuss it, the richer we will be."

Having come fully awake, and as if he hadn't heard a word Margaret said, he asked if he had missed lunch. Knowing Santa was confused, she told him, "Why don't we head for the dining room? Mildred's dinner is just about ready, and since you missed lunch, I know you must be hungry."

On their way to the dining room Santa asked Margaret if she remembered what it was she would like to discuss with him.

Choosing her words carefully she started by relating facts unknown to him about her childhood. Reminiscing, Margaret pictured musical notes floating through the air, and once again, they reminded her of the beautiful music she heard at St. Adeline's as she attended the services. It was then she remembered what it was she wanted to discuss with Santa; that which she felt was absent in her life at this point, and possibly had been for a long time . . . for at least as long as she knew him.

Feeling uncertain about which approach she wanted to take in relating the facts to him, she began with her presence in the barn while observing the Santaliers working on their entertainment program. To date Santa only knew of their work but he had not heard any type of production, so Margaret went on to give Santa a specific type of introduction.

"Well, you see, Sweetheart," said Margaret, "today I happened to wander out to the barn. I've forgotten why, but that's unimportant. What's important is the reflection the children conveyed as they were rehearsing their program. The sounds were simply marvelous and all of that from a guitar and harmonica accompanying the voices of Patrick and Gerald, with the girls providing their magical harmony in the background. For a moment, the music almost put me in a trance; I had visitors I haven't had since I was a little girl, and for some reason, they transported my imagination to St. Adeline's. When I realized I hadn't been there in years, I knew something was missing.

St. Adeline's is the school I attended before going on to middle school. Of course, the last term of my education was not in a private school; it was in a public school, and along with the public school came the absence of going to church on Sundays.

That's what the music in the barn did for me today. It reminded me that . . . , as much as I love you and my life in Santa Land, while I have no regrets, I know there is something missing in my life, and that is what hearing the music by the Santaliers seemed to be telling me in no uncertain terms."

Listening on the same level as Margaret, Santa understood what she was telling him, and before she could say another word, he asked her, "Margaret, what do you think about building a church in Santa Land? We have more than enough space, and to be honest, I recently discussed this very possibility with Alex, but I also told him I would sleep on the matter; well, I've slept long enough . . . the time for action is here and now."

Hardly being able to believe what she'd heard, Margaret knew she and Santa were traveling on the same track. Their idea was being thrust into one mission . . . . building a church.

Since enthusiasm was the mood of the moment, Santa told Margaret, "Hon, you know . . . , just the other day, when I mentioned this very subject to Alex . . ."

Anxiously, Margaret interrupted inquiring, "And what did he say?"

Thinking back of their conversation, Santa proclaimed, "I remember telling him . . ., that is my last words were, "Let's sleep on the matter; maybe I can dream up a solution; but Margaret don't you see . . . you confirmed the solution by solidifying my thoughts . . . and my imagination. Sweetheart, you are a Godsend, and as soon as we get home, we will start building that church . . . Its name shall be called 'St. Gabriel's Angelic Realm'."

Not quite understanding what Santa was trying to profess, she mystically said to herself, "It will become . . .

ST GABRIEL'S ANGELIC REALM"

FULL SWING

CHAPTER TEN

Three more days followed, and not a single applicant came to the door. The time to return to Santa Land became apparent.

While feeling depressed, Santa was not going to allow the absence of applicants to attack his spirit.

Wondering what he could do to revive his personal mood, he began to think of the performers of which he'd heard, but had never had an opportunity to observe. It was then he decided that he should have them give an audition for the remainder of the household. It would be, a sort of concert style presentation, not really an audition per se', showing everyone what they were in the process of developing and also, to allow their capabilities some habit performing exercises.

Of course, this was another spur of the moment idea, but with Santa, what else was new?

Having developed this brand new concept, Santa looked for Margaret so he could tell her all about this innovation. She would help him decide where and how to go about approaching the Santaliers for a musical review without appearing to be overbearing.

Though the house was not small, Margaret would know best where they could set up a show area and perhaps they might even consider an audience; but where would they find an audience? Knowing hardly any of their neighbors, with second thoughts, Santa decided, even before consulting Margaret, that a pleasant fireside summary might prove to be inviting; but how could he manage this, he wondered. It seemed best that he talk it over with her.

Locating Margaret Santa explained the whole concept of this new idea? He told her, "I thought it might be a delightful diversion from our everyday humdrum way of life here in Ireland so . . . why don't we set a day and a time when we will spend the evening around the fireplace with the children entertaining. Hon, do you think you could arrange such an affair . . . that they might give us the pleasure of their musical talents?"

Santa knew Margaret wouldn't say no, so after asking for her support, he suddenly became his usual jovial self and without meaning to coerce her, simply asked, "Hon, when can you talk to them?"

Commenting Margaret answered, "Well, that depends on choosing a night when everyone will be here with nothing else to do. Why don't we discuss it at dinner?"

Of course at the mention of food Santa inquired, "And when is that my Dear?"

"Judging from the light of the sky," she told him, she thought dinner should be soon. I'll see if I can discuss a performance with them. They are usually in the barn, and if we are going to plan this event, it might as well be at once."

Being an action type sort of people, when Santa and Margaret made a decision about something, one could almost consider it done.

Knowing the children were not in school but most likely practicing in the barn, Margaret proceeded to join them, so she could have a discussion with the group before dinner. Upon hearing their music, the whole building seemed to be swaying to the beat of a song called, 'Jingle Bell Rock.' To all appearances, the 'Santaliers,' were really swinging and, with a smile on her face, Margaret entered the barn, listening as the Santaliers played on. As the song ended she clapped her hands heartily as Jayne approached her asking, "What's up Aunt Margaret?"

Complimenting Jayne on their performance, she asked how many songs they had in their repertoire. When Jayne told her they had already mastered about a half dozen to date, Margaret cautiously asked, "How would you guys like to give a preview performance one night in front of the fireplace? We could call it, 'An Enchanting Rendezvous'. This rendition will give us some idea of the progress you are making; to date Santa has yet to hear you perform as a group and he is anxious to see what type of program you are developing."

From the look on her face, Jayne was elated and couldn't wait to tell the rest of the team so she said to her, "That's a wonderful idea Aunt Margaret. I'll discuss it with the guys and when you set a date, we will be ready. For now I have to get back to practice. Stay and listen as long as you'd like so you can give us your opinion."

Again, not wanting to be overbearing, Margaret told Jayne, "You've answered Santa's question but for now I prefer to be surprised." Telling her she would relay her message of acceptance to him, she left the barn, listening to the next song being rehearsed. It was a beautiful arrangement of 'ANGELS WE HAVE HEARD ON HIGH.' This music reminded Margaret of Santa's next project, 'St, Gabriel's Angelic Realm'.

Goodness, she thought to herself. If Santa can get that church built by Christmas, 'The Santaliers' could to a midnight performance, as the choir. Oh how wonderful that would be.

Margaret hurried back to the house to find Santa making a list of topics he needed to bring to the attention of various people. He was very enthused about the church he wanted to build, and decided to look for Alex.

Before setting out to look for him, Margaret reminded Santa that it was almost dinnertime and why didn't he wait to discuss his plans with Alex when he came in to join the crowd. Telling Santa of, 'The Santaliers' willingness to perform for the household she added, "All you have to do is give them a date, and they will be here!"

Since he had intended to discuss this event with everyone at dinner, he gave this project first place on his list of subjects to be announced. Next on his list would be the discussion of sewing costumes for the entertainers; then he would need the feedback on the two men who applied as Santa volunteers. Last but not least, he would make mention of his proposal to build a church in Santa Land under the direction of Alex.

My, my he thought, so much to do, so little time to do it in when one is in . . .

FULL SWING

PROJECTIONS

CHAPTER ELEVEN

One by one everyone gathered at the dinner table ready and waiting for another one of Mildred's delicious meals. It didn't take long before they found a way to relate their experiences of the day with whomever they could get to listen, regardless of where at the table they were sitting. Conversation literally ran wild until Santa finally tapped on his glass to halt the flow of chatter.

From somewhere deep within, Santa began to expound while looking around, and out of his mouth came the words, "Ho, ho, ho." When Santa sounded a greeting of this magnitude, everyone knew it was time to listen and over the incessant noise grew a quiet, worthy of a speaker, namely Santa.

His intent was not to intimidate them, but simply to gain their attention, enabling him to deliver his message which began, "I have a great announcement to make . . ." and he went on to say, "Alex has agreed to oversee the building of a church for us in Santa Land." Not being ready for this announcement, Alex thought to himself, well, thanks Santa, thanks a lot. I thought you were going to sleep on the matter, but out of his mouth came his instant reply, "I am . . . I did . . . oh yes that's right we discussed it and it seems to me that you decided I would build a church for you. As a matter of fact, you even decided it should be called St. Gabriel's Angelic Realm, right Santa?"

Looking at Alex, Santa questioned himself with, "Now how did he know that's the name I chose for my church? I never discussed it with him, what's going on?"

At this point Alex spoke up and said to the group, "Listen, everyone . . . I have it on good authority that Santa wants to build a church, but he will settle for a chapel. After all, there are not enough of us to fill a church so after reconsidering, we have decided to build a chapel. It can still be called 'St. Gabriel's Angelic Realm Chapel', and it will be a fine useable building but simply not as large as a regular church. I might add, for the number of people we have in Santa Land, a chapel should do just fine; isn't that right Santa?"

Not knowing what to say, he simply and graciously answered, "Yes, that's right, Alex," knowing he would discuss it with him later. Continuing with the announcement of the performance to be given by 'The Santaliers'. Santa told them, all they had to do was to be aware of the date and time decided on and provide their presence.

Knowing that Margaret had produced the costumes for the 'Entertaining Elvestos' Santa was certain that she would design and sew what was needed for 'The Santaliers'. In the process of mentioning this project Santa encouraged the help of Mary and Dorothy. Of course, they were thrilled since the costumes were for their children.

"Now," Santa continued to Fred and Donald, "Have you had a chance to check out the backgrounds on the two men applying as volunteers to play Santa?" Much to his surprise Fred reported, "Well, we have a rundown on Mr. Egowrap, but regarding Mr. Jiltor we have a few questions about which we will talk to you later."

Accepting this answer, Santa decided he would take up the date on which they could have their rendezvous with 'The Santaliers' and since Jayne seemed to be in charge, he asked her, "Would you rather this performance be at once, or possibly in a month or two, when the weather gets colder and appears to be more Christmasy?"

Hesitating to give her answer, Jayne listened as Santa told her, "School will soon begin and I know, that as fast as she sews, Margaret needs time to prepare your performance garb, so why don't we say, in a couple of months. In this way, you will have more time for the preparation of your program, and everyone will be able to make plans to be here; as a matter of fact, why don't we do it in the middle of the month before the holiday? So much work remains to be done before Christmas this year, with Santa training and all . . .."

"Good idea, Santa," said Jayne. "It will be much easier for us to fit practice time into our schedule without losing sight of our homework, as well as school attendance." Jayne's handling of this project amazed Santa; her perception was so sharp!

Because dessert time had arrived, Santa decided to put off making any further announcements. His next step would be the meeting with Fred and Donald regarding their report on Mr. Jiltor and Mr. Egowrap waiting for . . . .

PROJECTIONS

BACK TO SANTA LAND

CHAPTER TWELVE

Knowing the occasion to begin the training of Santa volunteers was quickly approaching, Fred and Donald set the time for a meeting with Santa to be held the next day.

Feeling their urgency, Santa suggested it be held after breakfast and the three men were found assembled at the conference table reviewing papers Fred had written, describing the two volunteers.

The address appearing on Mr. Egowrap's application, verified that he did reside near The Toy Thrillers Store; he also had a good number of nieces and nephews as he claimed. His admission as to why he was volunteering seemed to be honesty at its best. Now, Mr. Jiltor's, paper held a big question mark, meaning that his application needed to be reviewed.

Asking Fred and Donald about the reason for this notation, Fred told Santa, "The reason for the question mark is, when we made an inquiry about Mr. Jiltor at his address, no one seemed to have heard of him or even knew who he was. If no one knows of him, or of his whereabouts, how can we get word to him about the training class?"

Thinking about this predicament, Santa agreed and told them, "You have a good point Fred, so I suppose it will be Mr. Egowrap to the rescue. Why don't you send a short letter of acceptance to him and we will maintain the training here at the house. We have plenty of room for one Santa; what do you say guys, are we ready for one man?"

To their surprise Santa also told them, "And I elect you two to do the training while Margaret and I return to Santa Land with Alex so he can start work on our new chapel. I will leave you sufficient cash to get by until we return. Margaret and I will shop for groceries, and you with your families in tact, I trust will make good judgments. We will not be gone too long, and by the time we return, the work that is cut out for you should be complete.

Fred and Donald were amazed that Santa was leaving them in charge to train even one unknown man, Mr. Egowrap. However, knowing they were already familiar with the program, they decided it would not be a problem. Having had this discussion with Santa, the two men set out to put a schedule together, whereby they could easily make Santa proud of the finished product.

At dinner that night Santa announced that he and Margaret, Alex and Alfred would return to Santa Land for a short time and while they were gone, he had put Donald and Fred in charge of Mr. Egowrap's necessary training, to become a volunteer Santa.

Telling the crowd more about their next return to Ireland, Santa reminded Mary that she offered to help sew Santa suits, and when they did come back, they would bring Alfonso to supervise. Santa also mentioned, "As you know he has tailoring experience, and it was he who designed and created Donald's and Fred's handsome salesmen's wardrobe.

Several weeks after we return, the Santaliers will give a performance called their 'Enchanting Rendezvous' and by that time I'll be ready for another engagement to play Santa Claus.

We will be leaving early tomorrow morning, if you have any

questions or problems, we might as well discuss them now!"

Not having any questions, everyone finished their desserts and as usual Santa poured after dinner drinks for all.

Advising Margaret to be ready early in the morning for their return trip to Santa Land, she reminded him that they had grocery shopping to do; so Santa agreed to put off their trip for another day. He found no problem with Margaret's request.

Retiring for the night, Margaret and Santa arose the next morning at the usual hour.

With Mildred and Margaret having prepared breakfast, everyone ate heartily, and all continued with their plans for the day. While busying herself with the preparation of a grocery list, Santa made his way to the barn to help groom his reindeer and, to prepare them for the next flight.

Knowing the time for lunch had come, Margaret went into the barn looking for Santa, Alex and Alfred, who were working on a special project.

Having prepared a smorgasbord luncheon, Mildred's combination of ingredients and treats meant there was nothing left to save; all dishes were empty, and this put a smile on her face and a warm spot in her heart.

Santa and Margaret went to and returned home from their shopping trip. They seemed to have bought out the whole store, but she reminded him, "We are shopping for two households you know!"

Of course, Santa agreed with her and as they brought the groceries into the house, she separated the items staying in Ireland from the ones going to Santa Land and asked Alex to load them into the cart.

Knowing there were only four of them returning to Santa Land, Alex thought that maybe they could leave the cart behind and bring it back with a full load on the next trip. At first, Margaret thought this was a good idea until she remembered all the animals back home needing transportation when they made the trip back to Ireland.

Consequently, Alex and Alfred loaded everything to be put into the cart, and as far as they were concerned, their preparation for this early A.M. flight was complete.

After dinner, the group claimed an early to bed night so waking at three in the morning would be no problem.

Knowing that the O'Hares and Gilpatricks were staying behind, Santa bid them farewell before he and Margaret retired. Fred and Donald assured him they would do their best to train Mr. Egowrap.

Having fallen into a peaceful sleep, Santa had no problem waking at three o'clock along with Margaret to begin their journey
. . .

BACK TO SANTA LAND

A NEW DILEMMA ON HAND

CHAPTER THIRTEEN

Fred and Donald were preparing to notify Mr. Egowrap about his acceptance for 'Volunteer Santa Training'. Asking Leon and Phillip to write a note of acceptance for Nancy to print up, Fred told them he along with Donald would deliver it personally. Wasting no time, Nancy brought the finished invitation to the two men.

Fred being asked by Donald when they should deliver the note, answered, "The sooner the better. You know Donald, this is a new experience for us and it might take us a while to get it down pat; the sooner we get going . . . , well, what do you think?"

After some hesitation, Donald inquired, "Would this afternoon be too soon?" Enthusiastically, Fred replied, "I think that's a good idea! Let's find the gals so we can tell them where we are off to," and they went in search of Mary and Dorothy. Having looked all about the house, they were no where to be found, so Fred commented, "Why don't we just leave them a note and we can be on our way."

Dorothy and Mary couldn't be located because they were back at the thrift shop they had discovered earlier in the week, eyeing clothing Dorothy thought could be used as appropriate costumes for the Santaliers.

Finding what she thought was a beautiful selection of

dresses for the three girls, Dorothy and Mary proceeded to look for trousers and shirts for the fellows. Most everything they looked at was well designed and, to their minds, perfect for entertaining. They faced only one problem; they had no money! At this point Dorothy asked Mary, "Do you suppose they will hold these items for us?"

Knowing how Dorothy's mind and imagination revolved, she said to her, "And then what? After they hold them how are you going to pay for them?"

Being the manipulator she was, Dorothy answered, "Oh, I'm sure Fred will give me the money."

Mary's only remark was, "Well, if you say so!"

Asking the clerk to hold the merchandise till she returned, Dorothy said to Mary, "Let's go my friend, we need to get home and return before someone else decides they would like to have this lot."

Finding no one home upon their arrival, Dorothy knew where Fred kept what money he had. Rather than waiting to ask him for the cash, Dorothy helped herself; leaving very little for Fred. She justified her action by thinking, 'our children are worth it, so why not'. It was obvious that, she was not thinking about Fred being given the money by Santa to use for emergencies. Leaving some spare coins for him, Dorothy pocketed what she took, and with Mary, started back to the thrift shop. Arriving as the store was about to close its doors, Dorothy and Mary went straight to the checkout counter.

Asking the clerk how much she owed him, it turned out, she didn't have quite enough to pay for the sale items. Deciding to barter with him, she found that she came out ahead, with even a bit of cash to spare. The clerk put the clothing in sacks and, Mary and Dorothy left the store as it closed for the day. Feeling quite satisfied with her purchases, she said to Mary, "I'll bet the children will just love these costumes."

Dorothy's remark brought Mary a feeling of discontent. After all, the children were not little anymore, and she felt they should have been able to choose what they wanted to wear; on the other hand she thought, the damage is done. Feeling guilty about what had just taken place, and thinking back, Mary argued with herself, knowing she should have stopped Dorothy; but maybe, if by chance this doesn't work, the store will take the outfits back and refund Dorothy's money.

Then Mary began to wonder where Fred got that money and, why did Dorothy feel she could spend it so freely on something they weren't even going to need for several months. Besides, Margaret was going to design and sew the costumes the Santaliers would wear, meaning Santa would be paying for whatever material Margaret purchased, so what was Dorothy thinking?

Suddenly, Mary had a thought to offer about Dorothy's purchases and asked her, "What if these costumes don't fit or what if the kids don't like them . . . then what?"

Coming to her senses, for some reason, Dorothy suddenly realized what Mary had asked and she wondered, "Mary, you know, I never thought of that. I was so caught up in the children being involved in entertaining that I got carried away."

Mary's only comment was, "You sure did!"

Then Dorothy asked, "Mary, if they don't like them, do you suppose the store will take them back?"

Answering her, Mary suggested, "Maybe we had better show them to the guys first, get their opinion, and go from there."

"Well, it's worth a try," uttered Dorothy.

Reaching home, they heard the group rehearsing in the barn, and that was where they headed. As they opened the door, Jayne caught their eye and stopped the practice to talk with them. Seeing her mother with a big, stuffed bag, Jayne asked, "What's up, mom?"

Offering Jayne the sack she held in her arms, she told her, "I've found something for your group that I think you are just going to love!" Inquiring Jayne asked, "And what have you here?" Thinking she was being very clever, Dorothy took the bag, turned it upside down and emptied its contents onto the floor as Jayne watched. Looking at the heap, she questioned her mother, "What is this?"

Feeling speechless, Dorothy answered, "Well . . . um . . . . Mary and I were in town, and we stopped in that store where dad got the shoes to go with his salesman's suit. They had all of these lovely dresses and, look at the slacks for the guys and the shirts . . . Don't you think they are worthy of a group called 'The Santaliers'?"

Having a hard time picturing clothing that could be called costumes for entertaining and, not wanting to hurt her mother's feelings, one by one Jayne, shaking them out as she picked up the mess asked herself, "Whatever was my mother thinking?"

Telling Dorothy, "Why don't you take these garments into the house and when we come in for dinner, we can try them on to see if they fit."

Feeling a bit of consolation she turned to Mary who was watching and remarked, "See Mary, I told you they would love them."

Hearing her mother's comment, all Jayne could say to herself was, "Am I dreaming or what!"

As Dorothy and Mary left the barn, Jayne knew she had . . .

A NEW DILEMMA ON HAND

RIGHT ON TIME

CHAPTER FOURTEEN

Back in Santa Land, Margaret and Santa watched as Alex gathered his comrades and looked over designs, which would allow them to begin erecting the chapel, Santa and he had discussed and agreed upon. The materials he needed were already stacked in the barn, ready for use.

While this project brought them a feeling of joy, the fact that Snapper and Mewpurr died when they were in Ireland, brought them sorrow. Evidently, Snapper developed some type of cough, and from all appearances, Mewpurr being so attached to him, died shortly after from what they considered a broken heart.

In Margaret's mind appeared a vision of Mewpurr and Snapper running off into the sunset. Discussing this with Santa allowed them to know it was for the best; the two were playfully at peace.

However, now there was Mitzi and her little ones to be taken into consideration. The sad side was that Snapper and Mewpurr were gone; the bright side gave Margaret two of Mitzi's puppies, and one of them looked just like Snapper. So, with one puppy looking like his father and another looking like her mother the problem had a solution. Margaret would keep them both and call the male Snappy and the female Furyna, or Fury for short.

This occurrence meant three puppies, Turdo, Pepe and

Stinker would be going back to Ireland when they returned along with Rascal and Tyrant, who had been traveling back and forth all along.

Margaret was certain that Mitzi would be delighted with the detainment of the two pups and she also felt, with Snapper out of the picture, it would keep her from missing him as they seemed to be devoted to one another.

Since they had already grown use to their accommodations with the other animals, Fury and Snappy appeared to be quite content in the barn.

Margaret felt she had the better of two worlds; kittens and puppies when she was in Ireland, as well as, one dog with two little ones when she was in Santa Land.

She and Santa watched daily as the chapel grew into a beautiful representation of what, without a doubt, would help fulfill the need they both felt was missing in their lives.

Several days had passed and looking ahead, Santa began thinking of the conversation he held with Alex regarding the search for a minister who would actually want to live in Santa Land. Hopefully, and maybe . . . he wouldn't mind asking around about an available clergyman, who could visit and perform the job at the same time. This meant consecrating the chapel and allowing God to come back into his and Margaret's life. As a matter of fact Santa thought, we are about to celebrate an anniversary and maybe we could have a minister remarry us, sort of like an epiphany in the chapel.

Looking for Margaret so he could explain his visions to her, Santa knew she would love this idea. Catching up with her, he expressed his opinions as best he could. Immediately, she enjoyed the explanation of his concept so well, she began adding a few thoughts of her own.

It didn't take long for her to let Santa know they should actually do a whole celebration; what she was trying to say, Margaret explained, was this: "A Reaffirmation Ceremony' would be nice and a Celebration Dinner afterwards would make it even nicer."

Knowing the chapel was almost finished, and they would soon have to return to Ireland, Santa told Margaret, "Hon, if we go back to Ireland, we can get supplies and alert everyone about our celebration. We can invite the Gilpatricks, the O'Hares, with the children, of course, and all of our Santa Land villagers; maybe 'The Santaliers' will entertain for us, and when it's over, we can all go back to Ireland for my next Santa Claus extravaganza.

Thinking over the whole project, Margaret insinuated to Santa at the same time, "Hon, are you sure this is not too big an ordeal for you? I don't want you to get sick again!"

Deviating from what he thought was on her mind, Santa told Margaret, "Sweetheart, I'm just fine. I can't think of anything I'd rather do with you or for you! So, are we okay? Are we going to do this?"

Immediately agreeing, Margaret said, "If that's your wish Hon, I'm with you all the way!"

Consolidating their thoughts, Santa and Margaret decided that while Alex was completing the St. Gabriel's Angelic Realm Chapel, he would ask him to put someone else in charge of the finishing touches. Santa wanted Alex and Alfred to return to Ireland with he and Margaret to bring everyone home for the celebration, which they discussed.

Having a friend like Alex was worth his weight in gold, and as Santa constantly warned himself, "I'd better not forget it."

By this time, Margaret asked if he was ready for dinner?

Jokingly, Santa remarked, "I was ready an hour ago!" Taking his arm she said to him, "May I have this dance?" Waltzing themselves into the kitchen, Margaret looked through the refrigerator and brought out some tasty leftovers; namely a goulash they dearly loved, a small green salad and some garlic toast. They devoured every bit of food that sat on the table.

Discussing their trip back to Ireland, Santa told Margaret they should be leaving soon, and he would alert Alfonso, Alex and Alfred, 'Weather Permitting'. Margaret's comment as she left the room to finish packing was, "by all means."

Getting ready for their return trip to Ireland, Margaret and Santa, supposed Fred and Donald were busy training Mr. Egowrap to be a look-a-like Santa.

As it turned out, on the day training was to begin, Mr. Egowrap showed up at the door with Mr. Jiltor. Fred and Donald didn't know what to make of this situation. No one had sent

Mr. Jiltor an acceptance note and as Fred said to his partner, "Frankly, Donald, I don't know, what do we do now? What do you think Santa would do?"

Trying to make something out of nothing Donald asked him, "Do you really want my opinion Fred?"

Answering Donald, he said, "Well, some advice is better than no advice." Jokingly, Fred continued, "If we're wrong, I can always say I took your suggestion, and your excuse can be, since there were only two men to train, we figured, you Santa, would want a back up for the backup." With this decision Fred and Donald accepted both men for their first training session.

As Fred and Donald busied themselves with Santa training, The Santaliers were busy practicing and contemplating what they were going to do about the wardrobe Jayne's mother brought home. Thinking the clothing could be turned into costumes was fine, but no one found anything that would fit.

Wondering how she could get her mother to return the merchandise, without instilling hurt feelings, Jayne realized this situation would be a problem. Pondering the question a bit longer, she knew Aunt Margaret, returning soon would know what to do.

Suggesting everyone try on the apparel, Jayne allowed her mother to realize that no one fit into the clothing and, maybe she should try taking everything back for a refund.

At first, Dorothy didn't like this idea, but then it occurred to her that Fred was unaware of the missing money. Maybe she could return her purchase and get the cash back. Then she could replace the money.

Partially explaining the situation to Mary, Dorothy asked her if they should take this opportunity to return everything to the thrift shop. She had not yet told Mary, Fred didn't know the money was gone. Knowing something was not quite right, Mary said, "It's worth a try my friend, let's go."

Observing her mother's conduct allowed Jayne the opportunity to feel a sense of relief; she told the guys, "Well, you can relax, we're off the hook.

With a sack full of unwanted items, Mary and Dorothy found themselves at the thrift shop. Entering the store, the two women hurried to the checkout counter.

Asking if he could help them, the clerk laughed when they told him they were there to return some merchandise they had purchased yesterday. Quickly, the clerk pointed to the sign that read, NO RETURNS!

Gasping, Dorothy loudly proclaimed, "That sign wasn't there yesterday; had I seen it, I would not have made this purchase." Backing her up, Mary asked the clerk if she could talk to the manager.

Responding, the clerk told her he was out to lunch but if she wished to wait, he would make her presence known when he returned.

Agreeing to his response Mary and Dorothy meandered

around the store when Mary got a wild idea. Whispering a plan in Dorothy's ear that might work, the two of them proceeded to pick out a variety of other items they would intend to buy. Taking them to the counter Mary told the salesman they would like to exchange these items for the ones being returned.

Having no problem with this idea, the clerk began to figure up the total or difference the ladies would owe him.

At that moment, the manager came through the door and as he inquired how everything was going he added, "Roy, I'm sure glad you found that 'No Returns' sign," and retreated to his office.

Looking at one another Mary and Dorothy felt there was nothing wrong with what they were about to do. Taking the lead, Mary asked the counterman outright, " Sir, when did you find that sign? " and he answered, "Oh just this morning. Someone left it on the shelf below and it fell into the trash; it had almost been thrown out."

Hearing this comment left Mary with the conviction that the act she was about to perform was anything but wrong; so telling Roy, "Sir, if you will give us our money back and total up the new purchase, we will no doubt owe you more than we paid you yesterday; so figure up the difference, and we will be on our way."

Glancing at the sales slip from the day before, the clerk took the cash out of the register and handed it to Mary. Once she had the money in her hands, she told him to check with the manager regarding the items they were returning and she commented, "Explain to him that we were unable to use what we purchased because nothing fit. Also, don't forget to tell him that, the 'No Returns' sign was unavailable and had it been there, we would not have purchased what we did."

Speaking her piece, Mary said to her friend, "Let's go Dorothy. This man has work to do!" Moving toward the door, Mary glanced back to see the clerk standing aghast, with his mouth open and his hands to his head.

As they hurried on home Mary told Dorothy, "You know, we'll never be able to shop in that store again!"

Agreeing with her she remarked to Mary, "Boy . . . have you got guts," and she responded, "Sometimes you just do what you have to do!"

With this thought, Dorothy knew that she had to replace Fred's money the minute they arrived home and this she did.

Upon running into Jayne, Dorothy told her exactly what happened, and now she could breathe easier. Continuing Dorothy told her, "Aunt Margaret will design and sew your costumes, and Mary and I will help."

With this explanation, Jayne asked, "Mom, do you have any idea when she will return?"

Responding, Dorothy replied, "I imagine it will be soon, there is much work to be done; costumes to be sewn for the group, Santa suits for the two men, your 'Enchanting Rendezvous' performance to be held, I'm certain they'll be back shortly.

The next day, as if speaking the words made it happen, Santa and Margaret landed back in Ireland along with Alex, Alfred and Alfonso. . .

RIGHT ON TIME

A NEW EPISODE

CHAPTER FIFTEEN

Having returned from Santa Land with Alfred, Alex and Alfonso accompanying them, all were delighted to have Santa and Margaret back in Ireland.

Donald and Fred could hardly wait to deliver their message regarding the training of two look-a-like Santas.

The Santaliers were anxious to talk to Margaret, not only to ask about the costumes she would design, but also to tell her of the now hilarious story about Dorothy's purchases at the thrift shop.

Of course, Donald and Fred had not recently visited The Toy Thrillers Store so there was no report of what might be happening in that area.

Considering all that was involved, everything seemed to be under control so, taking the next step, Santa decided to check with Donald and Fred regarding whatever progress they were making.

As the days flew by, the time to celebrate Christmas was drawing near and Margaret, who found herself designing costumes for 'The Santaliers' made a decision to shop for the material she would need; not only for costumes but also for the necessary Santa suits. Taking Mary and Dorothy with her, they made it a routine adventure, but definitely not to the thrift shop.

Having a conversation with Fred and Donald, Santa learned the reason they were unable to locate Mr. Jiltor was, since he was a friend of Mr. Egowrap, he was staying with him. As it turned out, Mr. Jiltor was not only a friend but also an associate of Mr. Egowrap before he retired. As a matter of fact, Mr. Egowrap had encouraged Mr. Jiltor to join him in applying for a Santa position. Consequently, when he received the note of acceptance, Mr. Egowrap thought it meant both of them, and he brought Mr. Jiltor along with him.

Suggesting the idea of having a backup to Santa, explained why they were training both Mr. Jiltor and Mr. Egowrap as look-a-like Santas. Having no objections to this plan, Santa was pleased with the arrangement.

Meanwhile, he remembered having asked Margaret to purchase enough material for two Santa suits, once Alfonso gave her the proper measurements. Margaret did just that and came home with the necessary materials, allowing Mary and Alfonso to work on the Santa suits, while Dorothy and she worked on the costumes.

With no time to waste, Fred and Donald set out to visit The Toy Thrillers Store so their communication with Mr. Tankeroo would not fall behind.

Upon entering the door, Fred and Donald found the store was half empty, and they wondered what was happening. At first, they wandered around, but no one came to greet them, so they went directly to Mr. Tankeroo's office. Knocking on the door, they heard a weary voice inviting them to come in. Slowly opening the door, not knowing what to expect or imagine who it was that spoke to them, since it didn't sound like Mr. Tankeroo, they were astounded to find it was definitely he. Advancing toward his desk, Fred asked, "Mr. Tankeroo, are you alright?"

Looking very tired, he barely answered, "Yes . . . And how are you fellows today?"

Fred's quick retort answered, "We're fine . . . but look at you . . . what's wrong, are you sick?"

Quickly, Mr. Tankeroo told them he wasn't sick, but basically he was sick.

Wondering what the problem could be, Fred inquired why half of his toy stock had disappeared.

Responding, Mr. Tankeroo told Fred, "They came and took it!"

Trying to understand, Fred again questioned, "They . . . who are they and why did they do this?"

Thinking the men might be able to help, he started out by telling Donald and Fred the whole story.

Mr. Tankeroo said, "It goes like this, and I'll try to make it short:

One day, a man walked into the store and struck up a conversation with Beverly, my cashier. The next thing I know, he is asking her out to dinner; looking like an admirable man, she accepts his invitation. Being a widow and all, she enjoyed the attention with which he showered her.

Having an over abundance of enthusiasm about our Christmas in July Program, she told him all about it. Raving on about how successful it was, Beverly continued to tell him how much better it would be for this next holiday season, the real Christmas.

Well, the next thing you know, one day he comes in with a warrant allowing him to collect all the unpaid for toys and before you know it, men appear on the scene and start taking them out of the store left and right. By the time I'm able to question him, he makes me an offer. He tells me if I will use his version of Santa Claus for Christmas, he will pay for all of the toys that are still unpaid for and replace them so the store will look full; and, as I sell them, I can pay him back, as well as keep the profits! He has given me several weeks in which to make a decision. If I don't go along with him, he will not bring back what he took; the store will be empty and who is going to shop in an empty store? To top it all, he is pricing the toys so exorbitantly, there is little profit in their sale."

Fred and Donald couldn't believe what they had just heard. At the same time, they asked Mr. Tankeroo what he was going to do and he answered, "What do you suppose I should do? Will Santa still come to the store . . . even if it is empty?"

Then Fred asked Mr. Tankeroo, "Where is Andre'?"

With this question he reported to them, "He doesn't come to the store anymore. He tells me he's afraid of that man . . . he doesn't have any children and Andre' also tells me he is bad.

He doesn't want to be anywhere near him. Of course, Andre' doesn't know that most of the toys are gone and . . ."

After this explanation Fred continued to ask about Beverly.

"Well," replied Mr. Tankeroo, "with fewer toys to sell and little business, I couldn't pay her; so she was forced to take a job elsewhere . . . a job this man found for her."

Speaking up, Donald told Mr. Tankeroo, "Don't make a commitment to this man, we will find a solution! We'll be back tomorrow, just hang on!" and the two men hurried out the door to report to Santa what had occurred.

Hearing the story put him into deep thought; but there was a statement that struck a note in Santa's mind; Andre's remark to the fact that he didn't have any children . . .

Tucking the statement into his memory bank, Santa told Donald and Fred, "I'll tell you what we're going to do. We still have quite a ways to go before the Christmas season actually begins. You can go back to 'The Toy Thrillers Store' and tell Mr. Tankeroo we will handle the situation. His store will have toys galore, the likes of which he's never seen. He need not worry, I will be there for Christmas. Now go quickly guys, we've got lots of work to do and, you are doing a great job. Thank you for an up to date review."

Looking for Margaret, Santa began thinking about his plan, but he wanted to tell her what he had in mind first, before he began deployment.

Knowing he would take Donald, Fred and Alex along with Margaret when returning to the pole, Santa decided Mary and Dorothy should remain with the children since they were back in school, and Mildred could always use their help.

Having explained his reasoning to them, Santa heard no objection; they knew that something urgent was taking place.

Having returned from The Toy Thrillers Store with a commitment to Santa, Donald and Fred listened as he filled them in about his plan.

"Guys," said Santa, "This is serious business. First of all, we will make several trips back home, and we will transport a cart filled with toys from our workshop to be delivered to The Toy Thrillers Store; but mum's the word regarding our objective. Even though the girls know we are returning home they don't know the exact reason and I would like to, as a special favor, ask you to, please . . . please. . . do not tell them about this situation. You see, until we know who this crook is terrifying Mr. Tankeroo, we aren't certain who or what we are dealing with. The only thing we do know is, he's familiar with Santa Claus and evidently thinks he can provide one of his own.

Now, how are you two coming along with our look-a-like Santas?"

Being pleased with this question, they told Santa, they're training was almost complete; all they needed was the final fitting of their Santa suits and they would be ready to go.

Then Fred asked, "Are we going to take the two look-a-likes back to Santa Land, so they can see our operation?"

Not being certain how to answer this question, Santa told them, "That depends . . . I have to delve a bit further into what's happening to Mr. Tankeroo. I know you've told him we are handling the situation, but don't tell him anymore than that until we return with the first load of toys."

Feeling he had everything under control, Santa asked Fred when the men were to be fitted for their Santa outfits?

Telling him the fitting would take place in the next day or two, he told Fred, "Maybe we had better hold off until we return from Santa Land. After we make the first trip, we'll go back and bring in another load of toys and that should be enough to fill Mr. Tankeroo's store for the Christmas Season."

Donald and Fred knew this offer was going to be a magnificent surprise for Mr. Tankeroo.

The next instruction Santa gave to Fred and Donald, was to tell the two men in training, their schooling period was complete. The five of us, you Donald, Fred, Alex, Margaret and I are going to make a trip back to Santa Land; when we return, they will be fitted for their Santa suits. This notion to the guys appeared quite appropriate, and they had no problem passing this information on to Mr. Jiltor and Mr. Egowrap.

Returning to The Toy Thrillers Store, Fred and Donald wanted to be certain Mr. Tankeroo would abide by their instructions to make no commitment and to assure him, Santa was handling the matter. At the same time, they told him they would bring Andre's braces with them the next time they visited the store. The good news, brought Mr. Tankeroo out of his doldrums and back to life as he knew it.

That morning, the entourage took off early in the dark of the A.M., and landing back in Santa Land, they were welcomed by their comrades. It took little time for them to find their way home and gather a few more hours of sleep, knowing the next few days were going to be hectic.

Feeling refreshed, with sleep having worn off, Alex, Santa and Margaret found their way to the new chapel. Entering through the doors, they saw an exquisitely designed wood carving with the name, St. Gabriel's Angelic Realm arranged over the entrance to the vestibule.

Inside, they found pews, an altar and replicas of angels overhead holding canisters where one could place the candles needed to give them light. Though it was only a chapel, a feeling of reverence filled the air, and hardly anyone spoke a word.

Knowing at once that this was where she wanted to hold the Klaus Reaffirmation Ceremony, Margaret made her feelings known to Santa and he agreed totally while proclaiming, "All we need is a minister to properly officiate our services."

It was then that Alex told Santa, "I think I've found just the person you are looking for. One of my friends from Ireland had an uncle who he thought might be interested in this job."

Hearing this news, Santa inquired, "Is he an elf?"

Alex was quick to explain the circumstance of the special relationship the two enjoyed before one became an elf. Hearing Alex's explanation regarding the individuals involved, one an elf and one a species like himself, made Santa realize it was workable. All it would take would be someone like Santa, Fred or Donald to approach this minister and remind him of his nephew Daniel, whose ambition was to become a clergyman. At a young age, he was taken into a new life, thus leaving his family, friends and favorite minister uncle back in Ireland.

Becoming a friend of Alex, Daniel now resided in Santa Land and enjoyed his every day with other comrades. With Daniel being able to tell Alex where to find his uncle, he thought Santa could send Fred and Donald out with directions to search for him.

Continuing, Alex hinted, "I'm not certain he would want to live here in Santa Land, but I feel he wouldn't mind visiting, if we projected the trip as a sort of vacation or visitation."

Listening closely, Santa was easily convinced that this could be the answer to his perplexing situation. This settled the problem of finding a minister to consecrate the chapel, as well as to perform their 'Reaffirmation Ceremony'.

The next problem would be the gathering of toys and it didn't take Alex long to get an assembly line working to fill the cart to its brim.

Knowing he had no time to waste, Santa declared they would start the trip back to Ireland the following morning. At the same time, before he left Santa Land, he advised 'The Entertaining Elvestos' to be ready to return to Ireland when they came for another batch of toys. He needed not only their talent; Santa needed their help for . . .

A NEW EPISODE

A BIT OF SHADINESS

CHAPTER SIXTEEN

While preparing for his trip back to Ireland, Santa was still thinking about the crook who had duped Mr. Tankeroo into believing he had a warrant allowing him to empty his store of a large supply of merchandise. Resounding in his memory were the words, 'Had no children'. Why did these words continue to haunt Santa? Then he remembered that he heard Mr. Jiltor saying he had no children. All he wanted was to get ahead; but the mysterious part was the fact that no one knew him at the home address written on his application. Once again, Santa sent his thoughts back into his memory in order to get on with what had to be completed.

Asking Alex to call a meeting of his comrades, they assembled right on time in the Conference Room of the post office. Having already been introduced to the problem, Alex took it upon himself to conduct this session to pass on the information Santa had relayed to him.

Alex explained the need to fill the cart once again when they returned from their next trip; this would allow the toy bins to be refilled with new items. This meant their storage would no longer be overflowing, and everyone could get back to work at a moderate pace.

After announcing that tomorrow morning would be take-off time, and they would be back in several days, the meeting ended.

Traveling with a cart and sleigh full of toys, the weather was turning brisk, but the group, Santa, Margaret, Fred, Donald, and Alfred enjoyed a smooth ride back to Ireland.

Since Alex had given Santa the directions to find the needed minister, he stayed behind to direct production in the workshop, as well as to get the chapel in order.

Approaching the landing spot Santa told Fred and Donald the toys should be unloaded into the barn and if they would ask the children for their help, it would make the undertaking a lot easier. Temporarily, the animals could remain in the outdoors, but the toys needed to be sheltered. Being in agreement, Fred and Donald asked if they should wake the children or could it wait till daybreak. Realizing this was a weekend, Santa told him it was probably safe to let them sleep in, as they would have all day to handle this chore. So, everyone scurried into the house for a few more hours of rest.

However, sleep was not in store for Santa because he still had the puzzling 'crook' on his mind. Without warning, Santa finally placed the last piece of the puzzle where it belonged; what he needed before he could tackle the real criminal, was a description of his looks and appearance.

When morning broke, and everyone appeared genuinely awake, Santa informed Fred and Donald of a mission they had to perform in order to solve the 'Crook Mystery'.

Meeting with them after breakfast, Santa advised Fred and Donald to return to the Toy Thrillers Store to get a complete description of the man who Mr. Tankeroo claimed came in with a warrant, allowing him to remove everything from the store due for payment.

Wasting no time, Fred and Donald set out for The Toy Thrillers Store. As the store was about to open, they hurried to make certain they were the first ones in the door. Evidently, in a better mood, Mr. Tankeroo welcomed them and invited them into his office. At first there seemed to be little conversation, until Fred asked Mr. Tankeroo if his so called 'creditor' had returned while they were gone.

Replying in an affirmative manner, he also told them what had transpired between he and the 'Bandit', but no commitment was made. Not being able to remember his name, Mr. Tankeroo simply referred to him as a 'Bandit Out of Bounds'.

When Fred asked for a more accurate description, Mr. Tankeroo tried hard to describe him. Feeling nervous at the same time, he gave Fred and Donald an inaccurate description of what the 'Bandit' looked like. When Fred asked him if there was anything particularly outstanding about this man, Mr. Tankeroo replied, "When I asked him the reason for which he was doing this, he told me he was doing it to get ahead; sometimes you do what you have to do."

Putting this statement into a compilation of other facts, Fred and Donald compared notes, and they both came up with the idea, they had heard this comment before. . . but where?

Once again, Fred and Donald, cautioning Mr. Tankeroo to refrain from making any commitment to this crook repeated that they were handling the situation, without telling him what they were doing. They wanted the outcome to be a surprise for Mr. Tankeroo.

With everything at the store apparently in order, Fred and Donald said, "Farewell, and went on their way. They could hardly wait to report back to Santa; even though the crook's description would not be accurate, the words he uttered, they were sure, would ring a bell.

Once back home, telling Santa the whole story, though the description was inaccurate, the words he used definitely sounded familiar.

Santa now knew who the 'Bandit' as Mr. Tankeroo called him was; he also thought he could respond to this man, without a doubt, in a proper manner. Designing his plan Santa told no one how he was going to handle the matter. Alas, even Santa had what one might consider . . . not a dark side, only . . .

A BIT OF SHADINESS

NO WAY OUT

CHAPTER SEVENTEEN

All the toys were stored in the barn, and Fred remembered Santa saying that when they returned from Santa Land the two men would undergo a fitting for their Santa suits.

Approaching Alfonso, Fred asked if Mary had the suits sewn, and his answer was, "They're ready and waiting. As a matter of fact," Alfonso added, "two men stopped by yesterday to inquire if you had returned from your trip to Santa Land. Telling them you hadn't, Mr. Egowrap remarked they would try again today. They seemed awfully anxious to be fitted into what they called uniforms."

As Santa and Alfonso spoke, the doorbell rang and telling Santa, "I'll bet that's them, just as I told you; they said they would try again today and they are probably here right now!"

Going to see who was at the door, Santa found it was Mr. Jiltor and Mr. Egowrap. Welcoming them, he asked the two, as he lead them to the living room, to have a seat in front of the fireplace.

Though Santa was planning on a friendly chat, the conversation he struck up led in an entirely different direction.

While the men seemed anxious to get their fittings over with, Santa was describing a vision for them of traveling in a sleigh and going off to Santa Land. Actually, neither of the men seemed to be interested in a trip by sleigh, but Santa continued with this approach, while insisting they simply had to try it. He went so far as to tell them he was going to return to Santa Land in a few days, and he would like them to have the experience of manning a team which they would fly themselves one day.

Both men shuddered at what Santa was telling them, but they tried to show no fear. They had come this far, and they certainly didn't want to spoil what they considered to be their takeover at this point in time. Consequently, they backed off, and with a change in attitude about the sleigh ride, agreed to go along with him on their first trip to Santa Land.

Telling the two men he was glad to see their change of attitude, he proceeded to explain that they would be making their first voyage tomorrow and should plan on being back at the house for takeoff by 3:00 A.M., the sleigh would leave no later than 4:00, 'Weather Permitting'.

Being unable to find a way out of this ordeal, Mr. Jiltor and Mr. Egowrap had their fittings and departed for home.

As Santa worked out his plan he said to himself, "The best laid plans of mice and men oft' go astray"; but it wasn't to be Santa's plan going adrift. It was what Mr. Egowrap and Mr. Jiltor thought they had going for themselves, which would definitely be dragging by the wayside, without their knowledge of course.

Early the next morning, Mr. Jiltor and Mr. Egowrap came to the front door, and Santa was there to answer it. Since their Santa suits were finished, he asked the two men to try them on as he wanted to see for himself, how it looked to travel high in the skies in a sleigh as a Santa.

The time to leave drew near; Margaret, Fred, Donald, the two men, along with Alfonso and Alfred, were all settled in the sleigh and the almost empty cart was hooked up tight, the way it should have been.

With everyone sitting back, waiting for Santa to call to his team with his well known phrase of, "Let's GO GUYS" they knew he had commissioned their move and suddenly they were flying high, like birds gliding smoothly and uneventfully forward to their destination.

The two guests were astonished that something, which looked so forbidden could be so harmless and inviting; they were actually enjoying the ride. However, this did not deter them from the continuing thoughts of a takeover. Not being able to talk privately, they simply sat back and enjoyed not only the ride but also, the picture their imagination portrayed when they were in control.

Arriving in Santa Land proved to be so wondrous, they could hardly believe their eyes as they hastened off the sleigh and were ushered into the castle for breakfast, prepared by Margaret and her good friend, Dolores.

Asking Dolores about Mitzi, Snappy and Fury, she told Margaret, the animals were growing larger and positively delightful. Knowing she had little time to visit with them, Margaret made a mental note to enjoy their company after breakfast.

Playing host to his two visitors, Santa told them he would show them around Santa Land after they were finished eating.

Mr. Egowrap and Mr. Jiltor were anxious to see the whole operation; after all, there was a tremendous amount of acquisition to be considered, but they weren't quite certain how to encompass the total attribute, especially since they were in what seemed like a different world. While the atmosphere was delightful, it was certainly not a place in which they preferred to reside. Consequently, they said nothing, but simply stood by and observed the action in progress.

Santa, on the other hand, had Alex fill the sleigh and cart with toys. He made certain 'The Entertaining Elvestos' were ready to leave and at the last minute, he arranged a meeting in his office with Mr. Egowrap and Mr. Jiltor.

Waiting in his office for the two men, Santa made certain that papers of importance were not lying around; finding those that were, he picked up and put into a briefcase he could easily take with him.

Hearing someone knock, he knew the men had arrived. Graciously opening the door, Santa welcomed Mr. Egowrap and Mr. Jiltor, as he bid them to take a seat in the chairs he arranged. Addressing the two men, Santa declared, "I've asked you to join me because I have some very important ideas to discuss with you!"

Of course, the two men were becoming excited at the prospect of this conversation with Santa, even though they had no idea at all what purpose this talk held. Having discussed it with one another before arriving on the scene, Mr. Jiltor and Mr. Egowrap felt nothing but positivity coming from a private conversation with 'THE MAN', Santa Claus himself.

Deciding to sit and listen to him expound, the two men heard Santa say, "To begin with, you both know why I ran the newspaper ad when I was looking for volunteers to bring some joy into children's lives. Beyond my wildest expectations, you two answered my call for help. I appreciated your efforts more than words can tell. When I asked you for the reason you answered my advertisement, you Mr. Egowrap told me, 'it was hopefully to buy toys at a discount for your nieces and nephews.' That was a very honest answer. You Mr. Jiltor, told me your willingness to play Santa was a need to get ahead, also an honest answer.

Now, here we are in Santa Land, and I have shown you the heart of my operation; a conglomeration I've been building for more than forty years. We all know, I am not going to live forever . . . I've already had one heart attack, and while I am not looking forward to another one, the inevitable may happen; if it does, I will need someone to carry on with all I have built and make it worth the time and effort I have put into it."

Mr. Jiltor and Mr. Egowrap began to quiver in their seats as visions of a multi-mega company ran through their heads. Santa they thought, was going to pass on to them, what they had been conniving all along to obtain. 'How sweet it is', they were thinking.

Then came the straw that broke the camel's back. They were not expecting to hear Santa proclaim, "It has come to my attention Mr. Jiltor, that sometimes, and I quote, 'One does what one has to do'." Specifically asking Mr. Jiltor, he implied, "Isn't that right sir?"

Feeling a bit queasy, Mr. Jiltor answered, "Well, that depends on what you are talking about, yet, for the most part, I would say you are right."

Addressing Mr. Egowrap, Santa asked, "And you too, Mr. Egowrap, wouldn't you also say, even though you didn't say it, "Sometimes one does what one has to do?" and he agreed with him.

"Well," Santa went on, "is it not a fact that is why you took Mr. Jiltor in at your address, so it wouldn't be known who he really was . . .? And Mr. Jiltor, isn't that why you came up with a warrant to steal Mr. Tankeroo's supply of toys so you could establish your own company, equipped with a Santa Claus; and you have now learned to imitate him for your own intentions, isn't that right? Well . . ." Santa continued, "I'm going to give you a chance to establish your own companies."

With this expose' Mr. Egowrap and Mr. Jiltor breathed a sigh of relief and they thought, 'here's a man after our own hearts.'

The question remaining turned out to be, was he really?

There were two doors to Santa's office, and as he stood up to leave the room, he checked the door behind him, making certain it was locked. Next, Santa picked up his briefcase and told the men, "I'll be back shortly . . . you have something to think about, and when I return, we will exchange not only ideas, but thoughts on how you could have done things differently."

The two men were totally flabbergasted as Santa left the room and turned the key in the lock meaning there was . . .

NO WAY OUT

ONE CASHIER

CHAPTER EIGHTEEN

Leaving his office, Santa went directly to Alex and told him how he had eliminated the prevailing situation.

Laughing contentedly, while Alex thought he knew what Santa wanted him to do, he asked him what it was he should do with the men once he freed them from his office.

Santa's comment was, "Do what you have to do. Perhaps you can put them to work keeping Fred's reindeer groomed . . . put them on the toy production line; they can take care of the grounds, clean the stables and whatever else needs tending; for instance, how about the dogs . . .?

When we return with the minister, and Margaret and I have our Reaffirmation Ceremony, after Christmas that is, I'll take them back to where they came from. By that time they will have had enough time to think about what they have tried to destroy, keeping only their own gainful intentions in mind.

Asking Alex if the sleigh was loaded and the 'Entertaining Elvestos' were ready for departure, he confirmed Santa's inquiry.

Forewarning Margaret that an early A.M. would mean another trip off to Ireland in the middle of the night, they retired at their usual hour, but forgot about the men still locked in Santa's office.

Waking in the dark of the A.M. and finding everyone ready

for flight, Santa suddenly remembered the men were still locked up in his office.

With everyone on board, Santa asked Alex to unlock the doors and hurry back to let him know the men were free. Following Santa's instruction, Alex found the two men beleaguered and forlorn, yet they eagerly sought the port from which the group was leaving.

Hearing Santa give his take-off signal, "Let's GO GUYS," everyone in the sleigh waved to the men in Santa suits on the ground as Mr. Jiltor and Mr. Egowrap uttered to each other, "What now?"

Mr. Jiltor wanted to say, "Wait . . . wait . . . !" but it was too late, and his lips would not release the words.

Following the two men, Alex jokingly said to them, "It looks as if you guys missed your ride!"

Still in a state of shock, Mr. Egowrap looking at Mr. Jiltor said, "Can you believe this? How did we allow this to happen?" Being in a bad mood, he merely said, "Bah, Humbug!!!"

Observing their behavior, Alex suggested the men come with him, knowing without a doubt they were hungry since they had missed dinner and he would see to it that they were served breakfast.

On the way back to the castle, Mr. Egowrap did not seem quite as perturbed as Mr. Jiltor; he even seemed to be enjoying the atmosphere.

Leading the two men into the Klaus kitchen, he told them Dolores would prepare their breakfast and when they had eaten, he would introduce them to their responsibilities.

Questioning Alex, Mr. Jiltor asked, "Responsibilities, what do you mean responsibilities?"

With an unusual choice of words, Alex answered him abruptly, telling them, "You see gentlemen, we in Santa Land are very organized. We all have chores to perform and these are simply the everyday joys of life we do to keep one another happy."

Speaking up, Mr. Jiltor asked, "And what are those?"

With a smile on his face, Alex answered, "Have you ever heard it said, 'A busy soul . . . is a happy soul'. Well sir, those souls are you. We are going to keep your soul happy by giving you chores to perform, and we will begin by allowing you the privilege of grooming the reindeer we keep in the barn as back-ups, for starters . . ."

Looking at Mr. Egowrap in disbelief, Mr. Jiltor asked, "Is this guy for real?"

While Alex was leading the men into the barn, Santa landed back in Ireland and carefully set the sleigh and cart with all it contents down on the ground behind the open barn doors.

The sun would soon be rising and as everyone hurried into the house the Entertaining Elvestos returned to the sleigh and cart to help unload the toys, taking everything into the barn.

Time was of the essence; even with the sun rising, the skies seemed to be threatening a snowfall. The next step would be getting the toys down to Mr. Tankeroo's store.

Nominating Fred and Donald to look for a horse drawn cart and driver for hire, who would haul their merchandise, Santa told them this could be done after breakfast.

Once again, sleeping arrangements had to be made to accommodate everyone.

Though the children offered to share their rooms with the 'Entertaining Elvestos', having grown to love the sweet smelling hay long ago, they preferred to sleep in the barn. However they made certain their costumes were carefully hung in the closet.

Working as a team, Mildred and Margaret fixed breakfast and rushed the children off to school. Before leaving the house, Jayne suggested to the Elvestos that they get together and show one another their latest routines after school.

Hearing this comment, Margaret knew she would have to finish the Santaliers' costumes so they could finally present their 'Enchanting Rendezvous'; it was time for them to be heard.

Since Mary had finished sewing Santa suits, Margaret could employ her help and in no time at all, the costumes would be finished. The designs she envisioned came to life quite nicely.

As the children came home from school, Margaret asked them if this was a good time for trying on their garments, which would enable her to make any necessary alterations.

One by one, as they stepped into them, they were secretly pleased that Dorothy had returned everything she originally bought from the Thrift Shop. There was no comparison to what Margaret, Dorothy and Mary had sewn next to the items her mother had returned, thought Jayne; their costumes were so . . . much more beautiful, as well as inspiring.

At dinner that night, Santa asked 'The Santaliers' if they were ready to perform their 'Enchanting Rendezvous', and if so, he would give everyone a date to which they could calibrate their calendars at the same time.

Voicing her opinion, Jayne thought they should do it on the night before a weekend; then they would not have to worry about getting up for school the next day.

Agreeably, Santa asked, "Which would you prefer, this weekend or the next?"

Knowing Aunt Margaret still had some finishing touches to apply, Jayne chose the next weekend and then asked, "Is that all-right with you Aunt Margaret?" and she concluded, "That will be just fine."

Fred and Donald, announcing that they had found and hired a driver to haul their toys to Mr. Tankeroo's Toy Thriller Store, left Santa suggesting they contact him in the morning before delivering their cartload of merchandise; also to be certain everything was in good shape for this delivery.

Knowing Mr. Jiltor and Mr. Egowrap were tucked safely away in Santa Land, they could not imagine any other problems

Mr. Tankeroo might encounter, with the exception of possibly, being minus . . .

ONE CASHIER

DESTINY

CHAPTER NINETEEN

Knowing they had a full day to cover, beginning in the A.M., Fred and Donald, after making one another aware of their sleep problems retired early that night; both minds were busy with the delivery of toys to Mr. Tankeroo's store.

Being the type of person Mr. Tankeroo was, Fred felt there could be a problem with his accepting delivery. He just knew Mr. Tankeroo would tell them he didn't want charity.

Nevertheless, having found and hired a cart and driver for the trip to The Toy Thrillers Store, the time was at hand for Alfonso's comrades to fill the cart with the toys from the barn. Before they knew it, Fred and Donald were quickly on their way.

Reaching the store as Mr. Tankeroo opened the doors, he was totally surprised to see Fred and Donald sitting in a cart loaded with boxes of what appeared to be toys.

As he walked out the door he greeted the two men with a "Good-morning," and asking, "what brings you two out so early?"

Fred's reply proposed that they were busy handling his atrocious situation. Feeling totally flabbergasted, as well as realizing what it was they were trying to do, Mr. Tankeroo replied, "But I can't afford this. Whatever were you thinking?"

Picking up from where Fred left off, Donald responded,

"Mr. Tankeroo, please understand, we are not giving you this merchandise; we are simply going to apply the cost of it to your newly opened account with Santa's organization called, 'Bits of Stuff and Toys Galore'. It will help fill in the vacant spaces left when Mr. Jiltor took all of your other items away."

Asking the two men how they happened to know the name of the man who relieved him of his merchandise, Fred told Mr. Tankeroo the story of the two men answering the advertisement, which was, 'looking for volunteers to become backup Santas."

Mr. Tankeroo asked if they knew where Mr. Jiltor was now, and Donald only told him that he had been detained in Santa Land, they wouldn't be giving him any trouble.

Realizing two men were mentioned, Mr. Tankeroo told them, "I know of only one man," he added.

Responding to his question, Fred told him about the two men filling out applications. When we realized both resided at the same location, Santa managed to figure it out. The only problem is, now we have no backup, and we just hope and pray Santa doesn't get sick; but we feel quite confident that he is in good health. At any rate, opening a toy account for you was Santa's idea, and when the time comes that you need him, he will be here.

Now, how about Beverly . . . do you think she will come back to work for you?" asked Donald.

With an opportunity to tell the two men what had taken place the night before, Mr. Tankeroo replied, "Beverly called to tell me, she was quitting her job; adding that, Mr. Jiltor had not been around in some time. Due to this fact, Andre' wanted to come in and visit the store; he missed his grandfather. Beverly also told me, Andre' said he would be brave and if Mr. Jiltor were to come into the store while he was around, he would stand up to him. Andre' will no longer put up with his threatening personality. So, I invited them to come in today, and we would talk over his mother's return to work as my secretary and cashier.

Showing their satisfaction with Mr. Tankeroo's comment, Fred also told him, "And Andre' will be pleased to know, we've brought along his new braces. He will have them in time for Christmas. Right now, we will have to go and pick up the second batch of toys."

Being surprised by this remark Mr. Tankeroo asked, "You mean there are more?" and Fred's response was, "We told you, we're handling the situation."

As the men went on their way, Mr. Tankeroo was heard to say, "Amen!"

Riding back home in the cart with the driver, while exchanging conversation, Fred and Donald admitted to one another "It sure feels good to do this kind of work."

Continuing, Fred said as he inquired of Donald . . . , "Partner, did you ever imagine us, being in this position today, with so much to be thankful for . . . a wonderful boss and . . . well it's like being on top of the world. Tell me Donald, is this our 'Destiny'?"

Answering him Donald said, "Fred, I think we are on the right track . . . but it's not over yet, we have a long ways to travel.

Upon reaching home and bringing the cart to the back of the barn, the Elvestos quickly went to work loading the cart with the remaining toys to be driven again to, 'The Toy Thrillers Store'.

While Fred and Donald were busy accompanying the second load of toys back to the store, the children still in school were about to start home for the day. Once there, 'The Santaliers' went through one more practice session of the performance they were about to give. Feeling they had everything down pat, they were simply going to relax until performance time, which was the next evening.

With everyone looking forward to their 'Enchanting Rendezvous' the children attended school the following day, came home, finished dinner and in short order, dressed in their costumes. Having gathered around the fireplace, shortly after dinner everyone waited for 'The Santaliers' performance to begin. As they advanced onto the scene, Dorothy was reminiscing about the garments she brought home from the thrift shop and wondering at the same time, how could she ever have thought they would do as costumes. In no way could they compare with what she was seeing at this moment.

With 'The Santaliers' in place, Jayne stepped forward and began her short greeting, saying, "I want to thank you all for joining us at this first engagement. We hope you will be delighted when listening to what we are about to perform for you. At this time, we have prepared a program which we feel is most appropriate, and we look forward to doing this many times in the future, be it for charity or maybe . . . if we are good enough, for financial revenue; and now . . . may I present our 'Enchanting Rendezvous'." The group sang beautifully to the rhythmic music of 'The Little Drummer Boy'. The crowd clapped as they enjoyed song after song and finally it was over as Jayne said, "And now . . .," with everyone waiting in expectation for more, "I'm sorry to say, that's all there is folks! I do hope you have enjoyed our songfest."

Being overwhelmed by the group's performance Santa told them, "You are destined for success and when it comes, you will know this is your . . .

DESTINY"

A SUCCESS IN THE MAKING

CHAPTER TWENTY

With their concert over, 'The Santaliers' began making plans to give more performances beginning with one at school before it let out for the Christmas Holidays, and one at the Mercy Retirement Home. Having checked with management in both cases, they found their proposal was well received.

Meanwhile, Santa was ready to do his repeat performance at The Toy Thrillers Store along with the 'Entertaining Elvestos'.

Though Fred and Donald were needed at the store to help with crowd control, Santa suggested they take time to find the minister, Daniel gave them directions to locate.

As it grew closer to Christmas, business picked up at the store, and the magnificent array of toys were selling, as if they were going out of existence.

Beverly, the cashier, was back working at the store, and even Andre' helped straightening shelves and filling in empty spaces as toys were sold or put on hold for pickup at a later date.

Waiting for his new braces to be delivered, Andre' kept a watchful eye out for Mr. Jiltor to reappear, but he seemed to have disappeared. Andre' continued to help out as best he could.

One day, when taking time off in the morning, as action in the store at this time was a bit slower, Fred and Donald were sent to look for the minister about whom Daniel had provided information.

Being in luck, Fred and Donald found the proper church in a short time, and they asked the church secretary to check with Rev. Howdy, the pastor, to see if he could fit visiting with them into his schedule. Being an outgoing person, the Rev. Howdy proclaimed to his secretary, "You know I have time for everyone, show the two men in!"

Entering the room, Fred and Donald not knowing how to greet him, waited for the Rev. Howdy to speak. Welcoming the two men, he asked, "What can I do for you gentlemen today?"

Feeling more at ease and coming right to the point, Donald answered him, "Well you see Reverend, we are in need of a clergyman who can come to our village and consecrate a chapel we have built and also, to conduct a Reaffirmation Ceremony for two of our inhabitants."

Carefully listening to Donald's request Rev. Howdy asked, "And where is this chapel you have erected and when would you like to hold this event?"

Continuing Fred told him, "It would definitely take place after the holidays."

Thinking about his schedule, the Rev. Howdy told them, "I have a fairly heavy workload, and I doubt that I can fit it in but tell me . . . how did you happen to pick me and my church for this project?"

Hoping it was okay to give him the source of his information, Donald replied, "Well you see sir, there is a fellow in our village . . ., well no, actually there is a child whose name is Daniel, and he says you were his uncle . . . his minister uncle . . ."

"Wait a minute," said the Rev. Howdy, "how can that be? Daniel is no longer with us."

Realizing the pastor was right, Fred knew Donald shouldn't have made reference to Daniel being in their village. Thinking out loud, Fred took over and rephrased Donald's statement while telling the pastor, "There is a child in our village you must meet before you can pass judgment," and then he inquired, "Do you believe in the strange ways of the Lord?"

Answering, Rev. Howdy stated, "You would have to know, that I, as a minister definitely believe in this reasoning; otherwise, I wouldn't be in this position of dedicating my life to all, seen and unseen."

This appeared to be an unusual but still apropos answer. The question hovering, could they trust him enough to take him to Santa Land and offer him 'proof of the pudding', so to speak. They already had one dilemma on their hands, and then Donald said, "Nothing ventured, nothing gained."

Knowing in which direction Donald was going, Fred declared, "Rev. Howdy, if you will just visit our village, and we will provide the transportation, you will be introduced to a world you would have a hard time believing existed if only described to you. If you believe in the strange ways of the Lord, then have faith in us."

Hearing the soulful passion in Fred's voice, the minister shook his head and finally said with doubt, "I don't know, I'll have to consult with my wife, and if I agree to go, can she come along?"

Looking at Fred, with the pastor waiting for a positive response, Donald told Rev. Howdy, "Sir, one more passenger will make little difference. If you wish to have your wife with you, bring her along."

Being delighted to hear this comment, Rev. Howdy replied, "Well we will let you know, and if you will, give me an address where I can get in touch with you."

Giving the pastor their address, they left his office and hurried back to the store where Santa had a full line of children waiting to visit with him.

Because there was no one to introduce the 'Entertaining Elvestos', they waited for Fred and Donald to return to the store before presenting their revue. Having arrived, Fred and Donald found Mr. Tankeroo had lunch waiting for the whole crew. With the thought of food, Santa had an 'OUT TO LUNCH' sign placed in the cordoned off area and the store grew quiet.

During his break from the children, Santa brought up the subject of a previous task, which he thought had either been overlooked or forgotten; namely, the letters to Santa with requests from children he was unable to talk to at his July initiation. Mr. Tankeroo admitted to possessing a basket of letters he had received and totally lost track of due to the escapade with Mr. Jiltor; but now he would go and retrieve them.

Returning from his office, Mr. Tankeroo brought not only one basket but three containers, filled to the brim with letters from children being unable to visit with Santa.

Apologizing for his negligence in forgetting to forward the letters to him, Mr. Tankeroo made known his position. As he had no toys to sell and no secretary to sort the letters, he had settled into a state of depression and had simply forgotten about them. Understanding his predicament, Santa offered to take them home and have his crew sort through them and do what they could to correct the situation. This would be a big job but it was all part of . . .

A SUCCESS IN THE MAKING

AMEN!

CHAPTER TWENTY-ONE

Eager to report their findings to Santa about the minister whom they were seeking, Fred and Donald put it on hold until they reached home.

Being tired from a hard day of answering questions and not wanting to make promises at such a late date, as well as playing Santa, once they arrived home, Santa suggested they sit down in front of the fireplace to relax and have a chat before dinner. He was anxious to hear whatever information they could provide regarding the outcome of his problem with the chapel back in Santa Land.

Not wanting to keep Santa in suspense, Fred told him at the beginning of their conversation, "Donald and I found Daniel's minister uncle, and his name is Rev. Peter Howdy."

Explaining to Santa how they asked the reverend to participate in a Consecration and Reaffirmation Ceremony they told him, "At first, he was hesitant. Finally, as a last resort," Fred continued, "we revealed just how we happened to learn about him. Having mentioned Daniel's name, he looked at us in disbelief; however, with a bit of disclosure regarding not only his, but also on Daniel's side, we could see the doubt beginning to fade.

In the end, we described a village like one he'd never seen and I think we aroused his curiosity enough, for him to want to come to Santa Land with us if he could bring his wife. Not expecting you to object, we of course, told him that would be fine.

The next step is for the reverend to consult her, as we also told him we would provide the transportation and will wait to hear from him."

Once again, Santa telling them they did an excellent job, asked that they bring this subject up at dinnertime to surprise Margaret; but then he said, "Maybe we had better wait until Rev. Howdy confirms his invitation to come along on the trip."

Fred and Donald agreed and, by the time this decision took place, dinner was ready to be served.

Even though Santa had asked Fred and Donald to hold off telling everyone about finding the minister, he forgot to remind himself. Out of nowhere came his announcement about a Consecration, as well as the Reaffirmation Ceremony to take place in Santa Land when they returned home.

Wearing a big smile on her face made everyone think Margaret knew what was happening before Santa made it public, but claiming ignorance, with Fred and Donald as witnesses, allowed her, though she was secretly overjoyed, to now contemplate what she would be wearing for this event. Being totally oblivious to the crowd around her, ideas flooded the area within her imagination.

Since Santa had become so distinguished in his red suit, she would sew him a new one to be worn only for show. Then she found herself saying, "Maybe I'll even choose several bridesmaids to join us, as if it were a real wedding." Dismissing her imagination, she decided it would be better to discuss these ideas with Santa first, and this she did after they retired for the evening.

Answering Margaret, in an effort to help provide her confidence, Santa told her, "Sweetheart, I am going to leave this whole affair up to you. Being deserving of so much more than I have given you and, what makes us such a great pair is my love for you . . . and your love for me; what we do for one another, for better or worse, richer or poorer, in sickness and in health, I'm yours forever."

With his comment sounding like a marriage vow, all Margaret could think of saying when he finished delivering his compliment was a humorous, "Ditto."

They fell fast asleep, only to be awakened in the morning to the sound of the doorbell ringing over and over. Getting out of bed, Santa said, "My heavens, who is that leaning on the bell and what time is it anyway?"

Realizing he had overslept, Santa knew it was getting late and he was due at the store shortly for another session with the children. Quickly he dressed, gulped a cup of coffee, as he ate a piece of toast and hurried off to the store along with Fred, Donald, and the Elvestos.

As he reached the store, it occurred to him that he never did get around to answering the doorbell; but someone must have answered it as the ringing eventually grew quiet. Asking Fred if he knew who was at the door this morning, he told Santa, he thought Mildred had answered it, but if she took a message, it was never delivered.

Returning home at the end of the day, the group learned that Mildred did take a note from a delivery person. Thinking everyone had departed, she simply held on to it so she could give it to Santa, Fred or Donald personally in the evening.

Having retrieved the communication, Fred glanced at it quickly and reading it aloud for all to hear proclaimed, "Thank you for the invitation to travel to Santa Land with your company. My wife, Norma, and I will be more than happy to accept your invitation, to visit and explore with you in this new and exciting area. If you will fill us in on how many days we will be gone, it will allow us to make arrangements for a substitute pastor.

Awaiting your instructions, I remain, Sincerely, Rev. Peter Howdy."

Hearing this bit of joyous information Santa said . . .

AMEN!

WELCOME TO SANTA LAND

CHAPTER TWENTY-TWO

Santa kept a list of 'Things to do' and Margaret would check it daily to be certain he did not miss what had to be done.

With only two more days to go before Christmas, he wrote Rev. Howdy a note confirming the date on which they would be leaving for their return to Santa Land.

The entire household, animals and all would be returning to the pole. Margaret made arrangements to bring back not only groceries, but also candles and flowers in abundance, to decorate the chapel for its consecration as well as centerpieces for the tables on which attendees would be dining after the Klauses Reaffirmation Ceremony.

Since it would be unusually cold, Margaret would arrange to have tables and benches set up in the barn, while the animals weathered the cold outdoors and perhaps if it was too cold for them, space would be found on the first floor of the post office, where they could stay.

Having what she felt was a unique thought, she asked Santa, since they had the larger of the two sleighs, would he like to invite Mr. Tankeroo, Beverly and Andre' to come along?

Forgetting about Mr. Jiltor and Mr. Egowrap still in Santa Land, his response to Margaret was, "Why not! I'm certain they would be interested in seeing what they are dealing with. Tomorrow I'll ask them if they would like to join us."

The day passed and Christmas Eve was finally upon them. Being a short day for everyone, families were busy with the celebration that belonged only to Christmas.

Santa had Fred and Donald deliver the invitation he wrote to the Reverend Peter and Norma Howdy, telling them to be at his house on the day after Christmas, approximately 4:00 A.M., which was takeoff time. However, the Rev. Howdy was totally unaware of Santa's mode of travel.

Having told his parishioners about the trip they were making and, of their return in several weeks, he introduced the substitute pastor. Asking the congregation for their prayers with regard to a safe journey, he bid them farewell. With Christmas Day services over, the Rev. Howdy asked his wife to pack their bags, which would enable them to get an early start on the day of departure.

Waking early on the day of the trip, the Rev. Howdy and his wife prepared themselves to leave and found a buggy driver to take them to Santa's residence.

As they waited for someone to answer the door, Mrs. Howdy began to look around. Seeing no obvious method of travel in sight, she asked the reverend, "Doesn't this location seem a bit odd as a take-off port. How are we actually going to travel?"

At once he replied, "You know Norma, I think you are right. We're not going by buggy, or boat, train or . . . how are we traveling?"

Again, Norma asked, "Are you certain we have the right address:"

Reading the paper in his hands, he repeated the address and told her, "It says, 137 Hoopla Street, Makover, Ireland." As he finished reading the address Fred answered the door. Greeting the reverend, Fred invited him to come in as he inquired at the same time, "And I presume this is Mrs. Howdy." Acknowledging that the woman was his wife, Rev. Howdy asked, "When do we leave for the station?"

Responding to his question, Fred told him, "Reverend, we are leaving in a short time and, if you will allow me, let us move on to where we will be boarding. I'll have someone get your bags if you will just follow me."

Doing as he and his wife were told, Norma asked him, "Sweetheart, are you certain . . . that is, doesn't this arrangement seem to be a bit unusual? Are you certain this is what we want to do?"

Trying to shake his uncertainty, the reverend said, "Norma, . . . be not afraid, we have the Lord on our side."

Jokingly she remarked, "Well, I hope He's not too busy celebrating Christmas . . . we may need some help."

With this comment, the Rev. Howdy admonished her saying, "Norma, you should know better. How could you say something like that? You know, deep down we both believe in the strange ways of the Lord; we have already discussed this subject."

Apologizing to the reverend for her lack of faith she replied, "Well Hon, you know I'm with you all the way . . . what will be will be!" By that time, the three of them reached the pad where the reindeer were stationed. The cart was securely attached and Fred had Donald summon someone to load their bags.

When the reverend and his wife saw the reindeer, their first thought was that they would be traveling down roads through the woods, and probably along some back door route. Next, they saw what appeared to be most everyone in the sleigh, ready to leave and yet, it appeared as if some persons filled the cart; mainly animals and children, evidently not desiring to ride with the other participants. As they came close to the doors of the sleigh, Fred introduced Margaret, Santa, Dorothy, Mary, the Santaliers and the others riding along with them.

Even though their arrival was somewhat overdue, there was just enough room left for Mr. Tankeroo, who was delighted to be there with one grandson, Andre' wearing his new braces, accompanied by Beverly, his mother.

The time to take off came so quickly the newcomers didn't realize what was happening. Thinking they would be traveling an earthly route, they were quite surprised as the sleigh and reindeer ascended into the skies after Santa said, "Let's GO GUYS!" Had they been given time to think about this trip and the way it was flying through the air, the reverend and his wife might have changed their minds; but it was too late to turn back. The only place to go was to Santa Land.

Eventually, with the ride seemingly safe and sound, everyone appeared to relax as they enjoyed the scenery with the stars glowing in their splendor.

Never in their wildest imaginations did the reverend and his wife, as well as Mr. Tankeroo with Andre' and his mother, expect this sort of treat. It was totally overwhelming, and unless someone told them to close their mouths, they never would have realized they were open, gaping at the amazing picture having been placed before them. Had they been told in advance what to expect, they might never have made the journey; but being absorbed in the sight, hardly realizing their new venture was about to come to an end, Santa Land finally grew a face as they found themselves on the ground.

Looking around, they saw the lights of the village a short distance away and overheard Santa say . . .

WELCOME TO SANTA LAND

NO SURPRISES

CHAPTER TWENTY-THREE

The first operation the visitors noticed as they parted from the sleigh, was the tremendous presence of little people helping to empty the cart of its contents. They all appeared to know what they were doing and where everything they carried belonged. Co-operation among the elves was an important aspect of their daily lives.

In a short time, Mr. Tankeroo and Rev. Howdy, after introducing themselves to one another, became involved in a meaningful conversation.

As Santa led them to the castle, along with their kin, Margaret explained that space would become available shortly for their occupancy. While they were waiting to be taken to their rooms, Fred told Santa he and Donald would show them around the grounds, as Ralph and Jake took care of the reindeer, and lead them to their stalls.

Proceeding with the team Jake and Ralph were confronted by Mr. Jiltor and Mr. Egowrap. Keeping a careful eye on the two men, as they lead the team to the barn, Mr. Jiltor took this opportunity to express his thoughts, and out came the comment, "Not some more! What do you think we are, animal lovers?"

Knowing the purpose for which they were in the barn, Jake to his delight answered, "We are doing what has to be done. Love it or leave it . . . but where can you go! You chose your path . . . you might as well follow it, maybe it will lead to something promising."

Knowing there was no alternative. Mr. Egowrap picked up an empty pail and proceeded to fetch some water with which to rinse the weary reindeer.

Taking notice of his actions, Jake found it worthy of reporting the incident to Alex. There was no doubt that Mr. Egowrap was a cooperative type of person; the problem was Mr. Jiltor, being a total opposite.

Innocently asking Mr. Jiltor if he would like to help with the project he was about to undertake, Jake and Mr. Egowrap listened as he commented, "Do you think I'm nuts?"

Using his common sense, Mr. Egowrap commented, "Well something is better than nothing. How would you like to change places with these guys; have you no pity?" thundered Mr. Egowrap. "Supposing you were one of these animals . . . wouldn't you like to be refreshed?"

Absentmindedly, Mr. Jiltor shouted, "Well try me, Dumbo, and let's see how you like taking care of me."

Taking him at his word, Mr. Egowrap turned the pail of water over Mr. Jiltor's head, totally deluging him in water and thinking it was funny while enjoying every moment of his gesture.

Being unable to cope with what had just happened, Mr. Jiltor lashed out at Mr. Egowrap while screeching, "You idiot! Don't you have a brain in your head?   What's the matter with you . . . what am I going to do now . . . you've ruined my Santa suit, and I have no other clothes; do you have any suggestions my friend?"

Knowing it wasn't funny, Mr. Egowrap still wanted to laugh at his image. Asking Mr. Jiltor if, he would like to have him replace the suit with his own, the response was negative.

Observing the action between the two men, Jake definitely decided, due to its significance, to report this incident to Santa. If he had to choose one or the other for a friend, it would definitely be Mr. Egowrap; he was much easier to get along with.

Making his presence known, Jake asked Mr. Jiltor if he would like to come along to where he could find some dry clothes that might fit.

As grouchy as Mr. Jiltor was, he agreed to go along with Jake. At least it would give him an opportunity to learn what was happening on the outside, and Mr. Egowrap could groom the reindeer by himself. Following Jake out of the barn, Mr. Jiltor tried to befriend him; but being a bit on the cautious side, Jake was not buying his friendship.

Seeing Fred and Donald in the distance, Jake called to them, and they halted their pace. Reaching the two men, he explained the problem and asked if they had any unused clothing, which they thought might fit Mr. Jiltor. They could see the situation into which he had been swallowed.

Telling Jake he would have to check with Dorothy to be certain she hadn't disposed of his old clothes, Fred went on; but left Jake and Donald with Mr. Jiltor. Hardly being Mr. Jiltor's size Donald stayed behind with the two, waiting for Fred's return.

Watching for his return, they finally saw Fred approaching

with what appeared to be a set of trousers along with a sweater and a scarf. As he came nearer, Jake knew he would have to find a place for Mr. Jiltor to change his clothes and found the closest rest room.

Taking the clothing from Fred, Mr. Jiltor expounded with, "It's about time, what took you so long? I could freeze out here in this wet, Santa suit."

Feeling this was just an act, Jake laughingly told him, "And then you would be a frozen Santa, with no havoc for fun; so let's find a place where you can change and then we'll get back to the barn so you can help Mr. Egowrap . . ."

However, that was the last thought on Mr. Jiltor's mind. His only thoughts were to form a plan of escape so he could return to civilization, as he knew it.

As Jake led Mr. Jiltor to the vacant convenience room, he told him he would wait outside the door.

Modifying his behavior, Mr. Jiltor politely thanked him for his help as the door quickly shut behind Jake and he began changing his clothes.

Wasting no time, Mr. Jiltor was thinking to himself, now how am I going to get away? At once a thought invaded his imagination and he knew what he could do.

Leaving his Santa suit in a heap on the floor after changing his clothes, Mr. Jiltor moved into a stall with a door that locked behind him.

Raising himself up on the cabinet surrounding the toilet area, he simply waited for Jake to come back into the room to look for him. He would see the Santa suit on the floor but with the door enclosing the commode locked, hopefully he would think Mr. Jiltor had disappeared. At any rate, it was worth a try.

Some time had passed, and Jake, who was still waiting outside the room decided enough time had lapsed and, what could be taking Mr. Jiltor so long. As he tried to open the door, it appeared to be locked.

Then he thought to himself, what if Mr. Jiltor is in trouble? "Oh goodness," Jake sighed, "Now what?"

Trying to analyze the situation, he began banging on the door but to no avail; not a word or sound could be heard.

Mr. Jiltor however, while still inside, standing on the ledge around the commode, thought to himself, now is my chance. I imagine he will have to go and get a key to unlock the door and while he is gone, I can make my move. Waiting for the banging to stop, Mr. Jiltor thought he would then be out the door and away into hiding. However, he did not anticipate what happened next.

Though Fred and Donald went on their way after delivering the clothing for Mr. Jiltor, they were returning to the castle when Jake called to them, announcing what he thought was a catastrophe in motion.

In order to help, Fred and Donald agreed to stand watch while Jake retrieved a key to unlock the door. It would only take a few minutes.

Fred and Donald stood quietly outside the door while Mr. Jiltor figured Jake had taken leave of the area. "Now's my chance," he whispered to himself.

Moving slowly toward the door and then trying not to make a sound, he quietly turned the knob on the lock and pushed it open.

Eyeing the door as it apparently moved, Fred and Donald watched as the Santa suit was kicked out the door. Looking at one another, Fred and Donald gasped but held their breaths, as Mr. Jiltor tiptoed out into the fresh air, not expecting to see anyone.

Then he heard the words, "And where do you think you are going, Mr. Jiltor?" said Donald.

Standing in fright, Mr. Jiltor admitted, "I thought I was all alone . . . and I was about to find my way back to the barn to help Mr. Egowrap!"

"Is that right," exclaimed Fred. "Well why don't you come along, we will escort you to back Mr. Egowrap and then, we will have . . .

NO SURPRISES"

ONE SHARP COOKIE

CHAPTER TWENTY-FOUR

Since there were so many people to feed, Margaret asked Dolores and Nancy for their help with the preparation of an elaborate dinner. The guest rooms were totally prepared, and all were given a suite in which they could reside.

The Rev. Howdy and his wife had already been shown the picturesque chapel and thought the name 'St. Gabriel's Angelic Realm' was quite appropriate.

In discussing this location with Norma, his imagination invaded his thoughts and he remarked to her, "I wonder how they ever managed to get all of these materials to Santa Land for these wondrous buildings?"

Trying to be clever she said, "Maybe the angels flew it over, piece by piece; you know how you keep telling me about the strange ways of the Lord. Well, He must have known there was a need for such a chapel and . . ."

Not allowing her to continue the reverend commented, "Oh, Norma, let's not be ridiculous . . . I know we talk about the strange ways of the Lord, but let's be realistic . . . they are not this strange."

With her ever-present tenacity she told him, "That's your story and you're stuck with it!"

"Nevertheless," Reverend Howdy went on, "I'm anxious

to meet this fellow they call Daniel; I'm sure he must be a look-a-like, and yet . . . he seems to have said, "I was his favorite minister uncle. Daniel is gone. How could anyone have the nerve to imitate a child we loved so much when he's not around to defend himself; I defy this child to tell me he is our Daniel. Well, we'll see for ourselves. I'll ask Fred and Donald how soon we can meet with him, and then we'll know for sure."

Listening to her husband expound over his thoughts, Norma said nothing; she didn't have to! With his determination, he seemed to have said it all.

The next question, "What time is dinner?" found the couple realizing if they didn't hurry, they would be late for the event of the evening. Quickly changing their clothes and finding their way to the dining room where everyone was chatting away, they took their seats.

Dolores and Nancy brought in the food after grace had been recited and helped fill requests. Santa gave a toast to the success of his latest mission and thanked everyone for their help in the production of his wildest endeavor. He knew they were on their way to bigger and better things, and as he said, "Thanks to all of you . . . we know in which direction we are traveling, and we hope we have strengthened the beginning of a tradition that will go on for years to come.

As you are all aware, the Reverend Howdy has joined us, so we can have our newly built chapel consecrated and this event will take place in several days. Once the consecration is complete, Margaret and I would like to have you join us at our Reaffirmation of Marriage Vows, also in the chapel with a reception to follow in the barn. It will be a joyous celebration after forty years of wedded bliss. We will announce the exact details in a few days.

Now, let's all enjoy a performance of, 'The Entertaining Elvestos'." One by one, the Elvestos performed an exhibition and though, with the exception of the reverend and his wife, they had all seen it previously, their acceptance was unanimous and their revue was thoroughly enjoyed.

At last, the evening was over and tomorrow, Santa and Margaret would discuss the details of the consecration and reaffirmation events with the Reverend Howdy.

Bedtime was lingering, but so was Mr. Jiltor, back in the barn where Alex had prepared a place for both men to sleep and stay when there was nowhere to go. Much to his regret, Alex had to knock on Santa's door before retiring to tell him Mr. Jiltor was acting up. He said he wouldn't settle down until he had a talk with Santa.

Being the gracious person he was, Santa told Margaret he would return shortly and followed Alex into the barn to see if he could solve Mr. Jiltor's problem.

Reaching Mr. Jiltor, Santa heard him shouting and raving for all to hear, or so he thought. Catching a glimpse of Santa Mr. Jiltor told him, "You know I could have you arrested for kidnapping and cruelty!"

"Not so fast," exclaimed Santa. "I don't think so Mr. Jiltor. You came with us of your own free will . . . isn't that right Mr.

Egowrap?

Let's not forget Mr. Jiltor, you falsified a warrant to steal Mr. Tankeroo's private property and willfully removed it from his store."

Replying to this remark, Mr. Jiltor claimed, "But I paid for the goods, and once I did, it became mine."

Taking an unusual stand Santa told him, "Look, Mr. Jiltor, if you can settle down and go to sleep, we will have a good talk about this in the morning to decide how we can come to terms regarding your actions and what we can do to rectify the problem. Leaving the barn, Santa told the men, "Goodnight and pleasant dreams to you."

Morning couldn't come too soon for Mr. Jiltor, but Santa took his time with breakfast. Finally, sauntering out to the barn where the two men were being served their sustenance, Santa greeted them with, "Good-morning, gentlemen. I trust you had a good-night's sleep!" To make it sound business like, he added, "When you are ready, we'll go to my office for a little discussion."

Under his breath Mr. Jiltor said, "Yea, I'll bet!"

Pretending not to hear him, Santa also decided to explain, "That is, after you finish your chores; taking care of the animals." Then he smugly told them, "You know, if the animals are not properly taken care of, they may not be able to fly you back to where you came from."

To Mr. Egowrap, this sounded possible and right; but Mr. Jiltor under his breath once again, said, "Bah, humbug!"

Because Santa had what he thought could be a valuable idea to discuss with Mr. Tankeroo, he returned to the castle to look for him.

Having found Mr. Tankeroo with Andre' and his mother as they were finishing breakfast, Santa asked if he would join him in his office; there was an important mattter to be discussed, for what it was worth.

Being impressed with the magnitude of Santa's operation, Mr. Tankeroo knew complying with his request was of the utmost importance. Going with him, they came to a place that looked like a storeroom on the outside, which turned into a comfortable office on the inside. As they sat down Santa brought the details of the question right to the point.

"Mr. Tankeroo," said Santa, "when I asked you on this excursion, I totally forgot about some of the element we have here in Santa Land. Although I have distanced myself from this problem, there comes a time when one has to deal with it; to make light of its asset, I must consider the good and the bad.

Now, we have two people who were detained in Santa Land during the last Christmas season. One seems to be good, and the other, shall we say, has a rough attitude, for lack of a worse description. You know one of this team to be a Mr. Jiltor, and the other man, with whom you are not familiar, is a Mr. Egowrap. I became acquainted with the two men back in Ireland when they applied as volunteers to become look-a-like Santas.

As I studied the facts, Fred and Donald relayed to me, regarding the incident at your store, I slowly became aware of who was trying to create the havoc that took place in your establishment.

Well, when I had Fred and Donald tell you I would handle the situation, I did just that. Consequently, both men were confined here in Santa Land until after the Christmas season when we returned. In this way they were unable to manipulate any further damage to the project we were trying to develop. My question to you is . . . , no wait! Let me explain.

One of the questions I asked both men was, 'why do you want to become look-a-like Santas?' While they both had good answers, Mr. Jiltor's response was the least obvious. All he desired was, 'To get ahead'. Neglecting to ask him how he anticipated getting ahead left us wide open to internal damage.

Ignoring the problem, promotes the question, how would you like to sell your store to the two men and enjoy retirement?"

Not expecting this type of suggestion, Mr. Tankeroo sat back, and feeling a bit of shock, repeated the words, "Retire . . . retire! What would I do? Except for Andre' and Beverly, I'm all alone. I would have to discuss it with them."

Then, quickly reconsidering, he said, "But, if I can afford it, why not! It's time for me to retire anyway. Maybe we can travel . . . let me evaluate the situation with Beverly and I'll get back to you. The offer sounds very promising; just like what I need, while not to forget, how I am looking forward to retirement."

As Mr. Tankeroo left the office, Alex showed up. Asking him to take a seat, Santa told him of the proposal he'd just made to Mr. Tankeroo.

Having heard the story, Alex gazed at Santa in awe, and responded nonchalantly, "You know Santa, you are one sharp cookie; but right now we have two men waiting to visit with you, as they tell me you promised to do."

Acknowledging the talk he promised to have with Mr. Jiltor and Mr. Egowrap, Alex returned to the barn so he could accompany them to this office as Santa sat pondering Alex's description . . .

ONE SHARP COOKIE

RISE AND SHINE

CHAPTER TWENTY-FIVE

Waiting for Alex to return with Mr. Jiltor and Mr. Egowrap, Santa began making notes about the Consecration and Reaffirmation Ceremonies to be held.

Returning from the barn with the two men, Alex entered Santa's office. As they sat down, Santa announced, "Well, you guys are in luck; I have good news for you. We are going to return to Ireland soon, and you will be transported along with Mr. Tankeroo, Andre', Beverly and the rest of the crew."

Hearing this news, Mr. Jiltor and Mr. Egowrap looked at one another and appeared surprised to find that Mr. Tankeroo and his family were in Santa Land all the time.

Seeing the surprised look on their faces, Santa continued, "Fear not; there is no retaliation planned, only good news if that is how you want to look at it."

Addressing the men, Santa went on, "I consider you the type that would welcome a challenge. Consequently, we are possibly going to offer you a proposition you will hardly be able to refuse.

Mr. Jiltor, way back when I asked you the reason for wanting to become a look-a-like Santa, you're answer was, 'To get ahead'!

Right now, as soon as I receive the authority to go ahead,

you will be given the opportunity of a lifetime; one that will fulfill your wishes. You too, Mr. Egowrap, will be able to play Santa Claus and buy all the toys you want for your many nieces and nephews, at a discount. This arrangement should fullfill your fantasy; tell me, are you interested?"

Sticking to his original proclamation, Mr. Jiltor replied, "If it is within our means to get ahead, yes . . ., I definitely would be interested. Quickly, Mr. Egowrap agreed with Mr. Jiltor's answer.

Confirming the fact that Mr. Jiltor still had all the toys he had taken from the Toy Thriller's Store, Santa asked what he was going to do with them.

Mr. Jiltor explained that he had anticipated selling the toys back to Mr. Tankeroo for the previous Christmas season, but because he was detained in Santa Land there was no way to contact him.

Santa, suggesting that he might be able to return them to the store for next Christmas, was told by Mr. Jiltor, "By next year the toys will look old, and customers expect new and fresh looking merchandise."

Wisely, Santa said, "Have a sale; a Christmas in July sale like we did last year. The one about which you claim you've never seen nor heard of."

Remembering, Mr. Egowrap offered his comment, saying, "I remember that one; they almost sold out the store." Following up with, "Look, Ray," said Mr. Egowrap, it's worth a try. You get to be manager, and I'll . . ." but he didn't get to finish what he was about to say. With the exception of this one occasion, no one had ever called Mr. Jiltor "Ray," which led Santa to believe the two were actually associates; a fact they had never admitted to date; at least to Santa.

With a knock on the door and standing right there, Alex opened it to find Mr. Tankeroo. Getting up from his desk to have a talk with him privately, outside the office, Santa told the two men he would return shortly.

Seeing Mr. Tankeroo back so soon, he felt an answer to the problem had been solved; sure enough it had. Deciding to sell the business, lock, stock and barrel, if they were able to come up with an affordable, as well as, a realistic price, Mr. Tankeroo gave Santa an affirmative answer. Knowing he had not only the upper hand, Mr. Tankeroo found himself in the better of two worlds. Believing they had moderated not only a perfect deal, but also a worthwhile compromise, Mr. Tankeroo felt his nightmare was over.

Re-entering his office and, with Santa explaining Mr. Tankeroo's proposal, differences were forgotten; Mr. Jiltor began to behave like a human being.

Wondering what was next and when were they going to return to Ireland, Santa explained about the ceremonies that were to take place. Telling the men it would probably be another week before they began their next trip, he also invited them to enjoy themselves and saw to it that Mr. Jiltor and Mr. Egowrap were set up with rooms to replace their occupancy in the barn. The pressure fluttering over Mr. Jiltor and Mr. Egowrap had disappeared. Santa suggested that the time to enjoy themselves was now because when they returned to Ireland, the atmosphere would promote only work.

Being unlike the plan Mr. Jiltor and Mr. Egowrap envisioned, they knew something was better than nothing; they did what they had to do, whether they liked it or not. They could see a new beginning on the horizon.

Next on the agenda was Santa's meeting with the Rev. Howdy. Setting out to locate the reverend and his wife, Santa's reasoning told him he might find them in the chapel, where else?

Hurrying right along and reaching the chapel, it appeared as if they must have gone elsewhere because neither he nor his wife were there.

Thinking they may have slept in, Santa returned to the castle. Finding Margaret in her office, since he thought she might be the last one to have seen them, he asked her if she had any idea where they might be.

The only explanation she could offer was that regarding the trip they made to Santa Land in hopes of visiting with their nephew, Daniel. Hearing this comment, Santa knew he had to search for Alex who without a doubt took them to where Daniel could be found. Thanking Margaret for this information he went on his way to look for him. Finally, catching up with Alex, and because he was alone, Santa asked if he had delivered the Rev. Howdy and his wife to Daniel's location.

Much to Santa's surprise, Alex told him he tried, but when

he arrived at where Daniel should have been, and I inquired about his whereabouts, Bronson, the friend with whom he chummed, told me Daniel was no longer there. Questioning where he might be found, I learned he was gone for good and wouldn't be back.

Being puzzled, I asked, "Why?" and Bronson replied, "As we were playing ball one day, the lunch bell rang; weird as it may sound, I saw a pair of wings sprout from his back, and he was gone . . . without even a goodbye."

Alex went on telling Santa that he didn't need an explanation; he knew exactly what had taken place. Though he was happy for Daniel, he didn't know how to explain this event to the Rev. Howdy and his wife. They had come all of this way, only to be disappointed in the adventure that might have allowed them to actually talk to him; to know Daniel was safe and that maybe someday, they would meet again. For now, the two could only believe in the strange ways of the Lord.

Having traveled all this way, the Rev. Howdy knew he had other purposes to fulfill; namely the Consecration of St. Gabriel's Angelic Realm Chapel, as well as, the Reaffirmation of Vows between Santa and Margaret.

The Rev. Howdy was ready to consult with Santa so they could pick the date on which the ceremonies would be held.

Wasting a day was not an option. It was important that they get Mr. Tankeroo and his family, along with the two new, would-be owners of The Toy Thrillers Store back to Ireland; time was of the essence.

With work to be done and the children, also having to get back to school, a date was chosen and everyone found themselves busy decorating the chapel, sewing wedding garments and preparing the barn for a reception. Establishing the menu left Margaret in total control, and Santa was proud of her.

The day for the consecration of the chapel had come. Every villager and visitor attended, including Mr. Jiltor and Mr. Egowrap. Following the consecration, everyone waited for the next ceremony to begin. One could hear, the rustle of the Santaliers preparing to engage in their performance from the loft, of appropriate hymns before, during and after the celebration.

To Santa, Margaret was as beautiful this day as she was the day he originally married her. Standing as tall as he was able in his newly sewn Santa suit, he and Margaret repeated the words, "I do," in unison, as the reverend pronounced them husband and wife. Telling Santa he could kiss the bride, the crowd clapped as Bernard and Edward played the processional hymn for the two leaving the chapel.

Going straight to the barn, Santa and Margaret were greeted by Snappy, Furyna and Mitzi, all wearing delightful, dog creations. They were ready to show their love for Margaret and Santa and that time was now, as an exhilarating affair became reality.

Mildred, having prepared a splendid smorgasbord, per Margaret's instructions eventually found everyone mulling around, awaiting the entertainment to begin. It didn't take long for the Santaliers and the Entertaining Elvestos to begin newly developed performances, which none had previously seen.

Alas, the glorious day turned into night and the night cast its shadow of tiredness throughout the atmosphere, causing everyone to think about retiring for the evening.

Santa and Margaret had their usual bedtime discussion, detailing their plans for returning to Ireland with their guests and, to get the necessary legal papers processed. Santa was definitely pleased with the situation between Misters Jiltor, Egowrap and Tankeroo. Telling Margaret, though his work had almost come to an end, he knew he had to sit down with Fred and Donald to discuss the business and the manner in which they would carry on, once he was no longer able to advise and direct a course of action.

Ending their conversation, after professing their love for one another, both Santa and Margaret slept soundly till it was time to . . .

RISE AND SHINE

THE REAL BUSINESS

CHAPTER TWENTY-SIX

During breakfast Santa again mentioned his plan to have a meeting with Fred and Donald about the return trip to Ireland. He knew it was important to get the two new storeowners, as well as Mr. Tankeroo and his family, back on solid ground, so they could complete their transaction.

To Santa's surprise, the Rev. Howdy and his wife made an unusual request. Telling Margaret at this time, because he had forgotten to mention it earlier, Santa commented, "Rev. Howdy implied that he and his wife would like very much to reside in Santa Land if I could find a place for them. Telling the Howdys I would discuss this with everyone at the meeting and I would even recommend it, since I feel the villagers would agree.

With a multitude of important matters to discuss, Santa after finishing breakfast, left to look for Alex so he could call this meeting regarding the essential business at hand.

Having been alerted to the importance of the next meeting, everybody promptly assembled in the conference room of the post office.

While it seemed as if there were many subjects to be taken into consideration, the first was setting the date for their return to Ireland. Arranging this time would allow them to know just how many hours would be available for whatever had to be finished.

Next Santa asked about the Rev. Howdy and his wife, deciding, or wanting that is, to stay in Santa Land permanently. Of course, with everyone's approval, Santa then thought it might be nice if the village had an inn.

With the mention of an inn, Alex looked at Santa and said, "Whoa there . . . if we build an inn, who's going to manage it?"

Not thinking, Santa immediately suggested the Rev. Howdy along with his wife since they had the desire to stay here anyway.

In reality, Alex wasn't quite so concerned about who would be managing the inn as he was to its structure. Would Gabriel really want him to take on this type of building? Well, time will tell, he thought to himself as Santa continued to discuss other ideas.

Another one of his suggestions involved the recruitment of more elves. Of course, this question was directed not only to Alex, but also to Alfonso and Alfred, knowing they had many friends back in Ireland who chose not to make the original journey. Possibly this time, with a bit of encouragement, they may have changed their minds.

Santa told everyone about the contract to take place between Misters Jiltor, Egowrap and Tankeroo, so it was important to get them back to Ireland as quickly as possible.

Expressing his thankfulness for the work Alex's comrades had put forth in the production of toys, Santa particularly noted that this enabled them to keep the storage area full and ready for delivery on demand.

Everyone appeared to be content and with Santa expecting a new inn, he felt at this time he might include tourism for a real place of fun and how about an amusement park, for people to enjoy themselves, away from the Christmas Season.

Ovations for the plans Santa had in mind allowed him to believe, all of these ventures were a part of his destiny.

Remembering that he and Margaret were not getting any younger, he decided that once they had given in to God's oblivion, it should be Fred and Donald who would take over what he had worked so hard to achieve, but he really needed to have a meeting with them to make certain of the final outcome.

Knowing Fred and Donald understood, Santa wanted to be certain they had the upper hand.

Having dismissed Alex's comrades when the meeting ended, Santa asked Donald and Fred to remain so he could make known the provisions that would send them into what he felt were the proper directions. In this manner, everyone could follow his plan for what he thought would be an everlasting organization, waiting to be developed.

Once they had discussed the details Santa had in mind, Fred and Donald again, found themselves entirely committed to his ideas.

After they were back in Ireland, they would work diligently to develop what it was Santa would someday leave behind. Knowing he was leaving them in charge, this legacy was one that the Gilpatricks and the O'Hares, for generations to come, would inherit from Margaret and Santa versus Fred, Donald and their families. Everything had to be put into a proper perspective.

Having grown into respected persona, Fred and Donald knew there was a great happening yet to occur; they just couldn't define it at this moment, so they listened as Santa explained what it was he had in mind.

"Men," he said, "Now is the time to plan for the future. Of course, you will have to start re-training Santas; perhaps you can employ the help of Mr. Egowrap. While he may have a partner, Mr. Jiltor, I feel quite certain, will handle most of what has to be done. This process will leave Mr. Egowrap to pursue other projects during the year, until Christmastime when he most likely will be playing Santa Claus at The Toy Thrillers Store.

Also, I suggest looking for a salesman to travel to other parts of the country. When the word gets out regarding the success of our program, there will be a demand for Santa Clauses. Considering this point, it would be a good idea to start compensating the men who will become look-a-like Santas.

Your program will grow, and at the same time you might hire a salesman who will sell toys coming from Santa Land at fair prices because they will be using our look-a-like Santas. Actually, these two men should travel in pairs; one will sell Santa's services, and the other will sell toys.

Then, we still have the Entertaining Elvestos to be concerned about. I would suggest you sell their program to perform, for a price of course, to Mr. Jiltor and Mr. Egowrap.

147

As for the Santaliers, when they are finished with school and are ready to start traveling, you can work out some of the monetary arrangements for them; providing this is what they wish to do.

Now," Santa continued, "are there any other particulars you wish to address?"

Thinking ahead, Fred asked, "Santa, when we get back to Ireland, shall we have Nancy draw up the legal agreement between Mr. Tankeroo, Mr. Jiltor and Mr. Egowrap, or should we send them to a legitimate attorney?"

"Fred," replied Santa, "That's a good question. Keeping in mind what we have recently experienced with Mr. Jiltor, his personality evidently has a good side and a dark side. I think it would be well to send these men to a regular attorney, and listen to me closely. Do not allow Mr. Jiltor to give you the name of a friend who just might happen to be an attorney; find one for them. As a matter of fact, why don't you ask the Rev. Howdy if he knows of a good attorney back in Ireland, perhaps someone who belongs to his church, who he would endorse? Remember guys; always try to be on the safe side.

One other thing," Santa added. "Margaret and I are going to remain in Santa Land for a bit, so I will let you take my big sleigh, which will allow us to exchange sleighs for the trip back. After all, Rev. Howdy will have business to take care of with his church before he can move to Santa Land, and we will help him with that chore.

Having decided the time to leave would be in two or three

days, "Weather Permitting," the group ended their meeting and alerted everyone to be ready for the next trip to Ireland.

Fred and Donald told everyone, "It's time to handle . . .

THE REAL BUSINESS"

JUST AHEAD

CHAPTER TWENTY-SEVEN

Saying goodbye to everyone making the trip back to Ireland as they piled into the sleigh, and the cart was loaded with children and animals, Santa and Margaret heard Fred call out, "Let's GO, GUYS!"

Watching the group being lifted, among the stars in the sky and out of sight, Santa commented to Margaret, "I almost wish we were on that flight. As I am sure you know, I'm going to miss those guys; I've become very fond of them. They've grown so much since we first brought them to Santa Land; they hardly seem like the same men Margaret. Agreeing with Santa, she also complimented Dorothy and Mary on their change-of-heart attitudes.

Without thinking, Margaret added, "You know Hon, we should write a book telling everyone about our experiences; after we have it published. We could sell it in the gift shop at the inn to the visitors traveling to Santa Land. I'm certain people will wonder how this beautiful area came into existence."

Agreeing that Margaret, had a magnificent idea, Santa, with his mind on sleep said, "For now, let's just sleep the rest of our night away. We can think about this in the morning!" With little more to say, Santa and Margaret found their way back to bed for the part of the night that belonged to the early light of the morning.

Hardly able to sleep, Margaret got out of bed while Santa enjoyed his usual display of colorful dreams. Finding her way to the kitchen, she took some paper from a drawer and she began putting precious memories into the story she intended to write. It wasn't long before she had completed her first chapter.

Having finally awakened, Santa came looking for Margaret. Finding her, he asked what she was up to and in a manner befitting an author, she explained, "You know Hon, if I write my memoirs, you write yours, and we discuss them intermittently, we could put them together into one book and finish it even sooner. Then we can return to Ireland, investigate what it takes to get it into print, hope a publishing firm will buy it, and voila', there it is for the world to read."

As the days flew harmoniously between the two, Santa and Margaret, putting words and experiences on paper as quickly as possible, finally brought an end to their writing sessions. Comparing notes with one another, they came to the conclusion that they had the perfect manuscript.

Asking Alex if he, Alfonso and Alfredo would like to accompany them on the next journey to Ireland, Alex considered Santa's suggestion, and then said to him, "You know . . . It's time!"

Santa, thinking Alex needed the time to build the inn, said to him, "Yes, it is time, so who do you think you can trust to put up a glorious building just as you would like to see it built?"

Not really understanding the statement Alex delivered, Santa decided to send it floating into his memory bank and at another time, he would ask for its real meaning. "It's time . . . ," he said to himself over and over; but no further explanation developed.

One day as Santa and Margaret were making final plans for their return to Ireland, he said to her, "Margaret, I do think Alex is promoting his musical talent; yes, I think he is working on a song called, 'IT'S TIME'; at least, that's what he's been telling me for the last few days.

Well, I asked him if he, Alfred, and Alfonso would like to make the voyage back to Ireland with us, since we have to look for a publisher."

Answering my question about returning to Ireland once again, Alex responded, 'It's time,' and, of course, I thought that he was approving of our actions. Telling Alex that we were leaving for Ireland in the next few days, he responded to my invitation, telling me Alfred and Alfonso would be delighted to come along."

Hearing this information, Margaret, told Santa she was looking forward to this trip.

The time to leave had come, and Margaret, having their bags packed for traveling gave them to Santa to place on the sleigh. Since Mitzi, Furyna and Snappy were already in the sleigh, Margaret looked around the kitchen before turning off the light and then hurried off to the traveling group waiting for her arrival.

Taking her place in the sleigh next to Santa, she said, "I

can hardly wait to get to . . ." and with what Santa thought was a slip of the tongue, heard her say, "our final location." Trying to understand, he thought that's strange, she knows we're going to Ireland; but Santa said nothing.

With Alex at the helm calling out an unusual, "IT'S TIME GUYS," Santa was certain in his old age, he'd heard him mis-speak. Instead of saying, 'Let's GO GUYS . . .' he said, "IT'S TIME GUYS," and before they knew it, they were off into the wild, dark yonder when Margaret realized she had forgotten their book on the kitchen table. Telling Santa of her forgetfulness . . . he replied, "Don't worry Hon, we'll get it the next time around."

Feeling so great about Santa's attitude, Margaret simply sat back and relaxed.

It wasn't long before a thick cloud of fog appeared before them, and Santa remarked, "My heavens, I hope the troops know where they are going!"

Hearing his comment, Alex asked, "Santa . . . do you know what I was implying when I said, 'IT'S TIME'?"

Searching his overloaded memory, Santa answered, "Well, I've had many a thought about your remark; at one point, I thought you might be writing a song . . . , and then I felt you were referring to this trip. I also had the idea that you might have meant it was time to join the others in Ireland. Now, would you mind telling me what you were really trying to say?"

A cool, calm and collected Alex, responded, "Santa, we've been together for a long time. You accepted my help, as I gave it to you freely; but the time has come when I am about to get my wings, and Santa . . . you and Margaret are about to enter into God's most radiant accomplishment . . ."

Listening to the two men, Margaret interrupted and asked, "Was that the cloud we've just passed through on the way to Ireland?"

Responding, Alex said, "Yes, my Dear . . ., it was."

To the surprise of all, Margaret announced to Santa, "Sweetheart, if we are about to enter God's acres, "I'm so happy it is with you Love!"

While making this comment to Santa, they saw a vision of beauty as Alex, Alfonso and Alfred raised themselves from out of sight by the wings that attached to their backs. Flying off together, the three called a farewell to Santa and Margaret, telling them, "The gate to enter lies . . .

JUST AHEAD"

"IT'S TIME"

CHAPTER TWENTY-EIGHT

Back in Ireland, Fred and Donald were as busy as could be.

While the Rev. Howdy was getting ready to relinquish his parish to be able to take up residence in Santa Land, Mr. Tankeroo was coordinating efforts to complete his transaction with his lawyer, Mr. Jiltor and Mr. Egowrap.

After giving the matter much thought, Mr. Tankeroo decided to put a clause into the contract, whereas Andre', his grandson, would inherit the business from the two new owners after their demise. After all, Mr. Jiltor had no relatives and Mr. Egowrap had only nieces and nephews, so why not?

Though Mr. Tankeroo, with the help of his daughter as secretary and cashier, had everything in tip top shape, Mr. Egowrap managed along with Mr. Jiltor to mess things up considerably and consequently, needed more help than he imagined. The two with full time jobs, began to organize a Christmas in July sale, but found it was not going to be easy.

The time for signing the contract of sale paper had arrived and it was delivered to the store for pre-reading. Noting the clause, which proclaimed Andre' along with his mother as guardian, until he came of age, was to inherit the business after their demise, Mr. Jiltor didn't give it a second thought; his cunning mind was fast at work with a plan to find help with his cluttered desk. The two men had settled comfortably into the destination of their lives, but it was not as easy as they had anticipated.

Having set the date to meet with Mr. Tankeroo at the attorney's office for the legal signing of the papers, Mr. Jiltor decided he'd better fill Mr. Egowrap in on the details. Once he accomplished this feat, he and his partner relaxed until the event of realization had arrived.

Meanwhile, Fred and Donald were hard at work trying to organize all of the tasks at hand such as, hiring salesmen, Santa look-a-likes, setting up procedures in which to train the men, getting the Santaliers through school and delivering the Rev. Howdy along with his wife Norma, back to Santa Land. With a busy schedule, Fred and his family never gave a second thought as to why Santa was staying away for so long; they simply felt he and Margaret deserved a rest, as well as an opportunity to be alone.

However, the day came when the Rev. Howdy and his wife seemed anxious to get back to Santa Land so they could reunite with Santa and set up shop.

A date for the journey had been set for Easter time when the children would have a longer than usual break from school.

Rev. Howdy reminded them that if they left in time, he would be able to give an Easter Day Service, so the date was set to leave for Santa Land four days before Easter.

Since business had been taken care of, Mr. Tankeroo, having been entirely relieved of legal matters, asked if he and his family might travel along with them; they were totally thrilled with Santa Land.

Feeling as Mr. Tankeroo, Beverly and Andre' were almost family, the Gilpatricks and O'Hares welcomed their participation, and off they went on the chosen date, returning to Santa Land.

Arriving early in the morning, the group was not surprised to find that there was no one to greet them at the landing port; after all, no one knew they were coming.

Filing out of the sleigh, Fred and Donald tended to the reindeer, as everyone else returned to the castle.

Expressing their thoughts of how great it felt to be back in Santa Land, while not leaving any doubt of their love for the life in Ireland, Dorothy expounded, "This is like our home away from home." Adding to the statement, Mary inquired, "Or is it the other way around?"

With the last word, as Dorothy habitually practiced, they proceeded to their apartments as she proclaimed, "It's so good to be here!"

Since there was no one to direct the Rev. Howdy and his wife, Mary said, "I imagine it's all right for you to occupy the suite you used when you were here last. I'll check with Margaret," and why don't you go ahead! I'll ask Fred to have your bags delivered to your room." Following her directions, the Howdys found the suite in which they had previously stayed and Mr. Tankeroo and his family did the same.

Being so early in the morning, Mary decided not to disturb Santa and Margaret; this surprise encounter could wait until breakfast.

At the same time, having taken the reindeer to the barn, Fred and Donald noticed that Santa's team was nowhere to be found; even Mitzi, Snappy and Furyna were not in their stall.

"That's strange," said Fred to Donald. "Do you suppose we crossed paths on our way back here, but didn't see Santa and Margaret as we passed them?"

Being at a loss for words, with Donald finding excuses for everything, he told Fred, "Maybe they're just out exercising the reindeer."

"Well, I sure hope so," concluded Fred.

By this time, Jake the helper who had become Director of Stable Care, found his way into the barn. Greeting Fred and Donald with, "A good-morning to you and how are you two doing today?"

Replying, Fred remarked, "We're just fine, but I'd be doing better if you could tell me where Santa's reindeer have gone?"

Surprisingly, Jake answered, "Why, they should be with you sir! They left several days ago with Alex, Alfonso, Alfred and the dogs. As a matter of fact, Alex put Russell and Punky in charge of building the new inn. It's up and ready for operation just as he requested."

Being unable to accept the facts as Jake was relating them, Fred and Donald questioned, "Are you certain their destination was Ireland?"

Responding, Jake inquired, "Where else would they have gone; especially without telling anyone?"

Answering him, Donald claimed, "But they never arrived . . . where do you suppose they are . . . ? What happened to them . . . ?"

Being affected by the cold air, Fred told Donald, "Let's go look at the inn and then we'll go to the castle to see what we can find. Maybe they left a message; I'm confident there must be a plausible answer to this situation!"

Jake directed Fred and Donald to the beautifully built inn and, Fred was, as Santa usually had been, amazed at its construction.

They did not stay long, since both Fred and Donald were anxious to knock on Santa's door; wondering who would answer. "This is unreal," commented Donald to Fred.

Going right to the Klaus residence, they found the front door unlocked. Looking around the neatly kept apartment, they were in suspense about what might be located in the rest of the quarters.

Coming through the door into the kitchen, Donald spied what appeared to be a stack of papers resembling a book on the table. Walking over to look at the papers, he noticed upon the first page was written what appeared to be a title, 'SANTA KLAUS vs. SANTA CLAUS'.

"Well, I'll be," uttered Fred as he flipped through the pages. Realizing their whole story had been put on paper, he questioned, "But why didn't they take it along?"

Questions and more questions abounded when there was a knock on the door. Answering it, Donald found Jake ready to offer them some information and reason as to what he thought could be credible evidence regarding what might have taken place.

Jake told them . . . "For sometime, Alex had been heard repeating the words, 'It's time . . . It's time'. No one knew what it meant and then, recently after they left on their last journey, someone found a book of Irish Proverbs. In this book could be found the words, 'IT'S TIME . . .'!

The explanation for 'IT'S TIME' reads:

When someone who has a strong faith in the Lord verbally continues to repeat , 'IT'S TIME' , it means a great happening is about to take place . . . and 'IT'S TIME' is defined as, 'HAPPENING NOW' ."

Though Fred and Donald needed to think about this explanation, they knew something strange had taken place; but then, hadn't strange things always taken place . . .? Isn't that why Santa and Margaret believed so in 'THE STRANGE WAYS OF

THE LORD'?

It was time to break the news to their families and the villagers. There was so much work to be done . . . the responsibility was all theirs, and it was evident, the time had come.

The time had come . . . the time was now; and they knew
as Fred and Donald looked at one another and, with their lips in
synchronization, whispered . . . .

"IT'S TIME"

Irene Zulueta

It's Time

It's time to smell the roses,
It's time to call it a day.
When all the happiness glowing,
Is no longer here to stay.
A light is always beaming
Leading us on our way,
To a heaven lit up so brightly,
An aura on display
Our love will live forever,
Wherever we may be.
So love me as I love you,
It's time to call it a day.

The angels hovering near us,
Will help to show us the way.
For God has truly assured us,
Our projects were for yesterday.
Our friends will soon be with us,
They'll find we did not stray,
And when we greet one another,
We'll gladly hear them say,
"Where have you been, we've missed you?
Wherever do you play?
We'll tell them, "Come along with us,
It's time to call it a day!"

Look for
MARGARET'S LUCKY IRISH TREE
in 2010

Order Blank

For additional copies of the following books send check or money order to :

ECHOED VISIONS
P.O. BOX 97
SUN CITY, CA 92586-3757

_____ Christmas Fantasy @ $11.95 _____

_____ Santa's In-Between Years @ $14.95 _____

_____ Santa's Second Chance @ $14.95 _____

_____ Santa's Greatest Pursuit @ $14.95 _____

Shipping & Handling $5.00

Total _____

Name _____

Address _____

City, ST Zip _____

(no credit cards please)

Look for the coming book

Margaret's Lucky Irish Tree

available in 2010